Dear Reader,

What's the answer to stress? Chocolate. More stress? More chocolate.

Last fall, as I was eating a pan of brownies after a long day at work, I contemplated what would happen if chocolate disappeared from the planet and I still had to go to work and pretend to be sane. My imagination promptly took off, and soon I had the story of Cassie Halloway, a stress-management therapist with a need for chocolate. Throw in a hot guy with a fiancée and some delusions about love, and you've got *Stress & the City*.

I've always been willing to sacrifice my reputation for a bit of levity. What's pride if you can brighten someone's day? Writing for Harlequin Flipside allows my true self to emerge: having in-depth conversations with imaginary people, laughing out loud at things only I hear and being able to share them with you. I'm so excited to be a part of Flipside.

The fact that this book won the Romance Writers of America Golden Heart award and caught my editor's eye (there was no bribery involved, I swear!) gives me hope that you, too, might find yourself laughing at Cassie's view of the world and climbing on board with her as she goes after true love.

Happy reading!

Stephanie Rowe

It was official. She'd totally and completely lost all grip on reality and sanity...

Okay, so Cassie had freaked out. It was over. No one had seen it and it was behind her now. It was a cathartic episode she'd obviously needed, but now that she'd had her release, she'd be fine.

From this moment on, she'd be in complete control of her emotions. Calm, controlled and dignified. Reserved, even. People would start calling her the Cucumber because she was so cool.

The Cucumber could handle rejection.

The Cucumber wouldn't freak if a man stood her up.

The Cucumber could separate the wreck of her soul from her professional life....

Next agenda item for the Cucumber? Deal with the elusive Ty Parker. He thought he could outwit her by following through on his refusal to meet her today?

Hah. He had no idea who he was dealing with. "Ty, better get ready for battle. The Cucumber is not easily dismissed."

Stress & the City

Stephanie Rowe

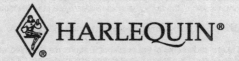

HARLEQUIN®

TORONTO • NEW YORK • LONDON
AMSTERDAM • PARIS • SYDNEY • HAMBURG
STOCKHOLM • ATHENS • TOKYO • MILAN • MADRID
PRAGUE • WARSAW • BUDAPEST • AUCKLAND

ISBN 0-373-44187-8

STRESS & THE CITY

Visit us at www.eHarlequin.com

Printed in U.S.A.

ABOUT THE AUTHOR

A lifelong reader of romance, Golden Heart winner Stephanie Rowe wrote her first novel when she was ten and sold her first book twenty-three years later. After experimenting with a legal career, she decided wearing suits wasn't her style and opted for a more fulfilling career entertaining herself and others with stories of romance, humor and, of course, true love. She currently shares her household with two dogs, two cats and her own hero. When not glued to the computer or avoiding housework, she can be found on the tennis court, reading or inviting herself over to her mom's house for dinner. You can reach her at www.stephanierowe.com.

To Mom and Dad, for teaching me
I could do anything and for giving me the skills
to prove them right.

To Josh, for everything.

To my wonderful agent, Michelle Grajkowski,
and fabulous editor, Wanda Ottewell.
How do I thank you enough for believing in me?

1

"I'M PROUD OF THE FACT I took my honeymoon by myself," Cassie Halloway announced as she selected an oversize piece of chocolate from the refreshment table. Only three hours off the plane and somehow she'd allowed her best friend, Leonore—better known as Leo—Wethers, to drag her to Gardenbloom, Connecticut's New Year's Eve dance. Now that she was here, she regretted her foolish moment of malleability. Not that she didn't like dances, but it had been so much easier to deny the reality of her life when she was hovering alone by the hotel pool, pretending the puffiness of her bloodshot eyes was actually a new beauty regime highly sought after by New York socialites.

"You should be impressed with yourself," Leo agreed. "Taking a solo honeymoon is definitely an accomplishment most women can only dream of."

"Poor deprived souls. I pity them." Just about everyone Cassie knew in town was here, plus some she didn't.

Too many people.

Too much noise.

She needed help.

So she broke off a piece of fudge and placed it on her tongue, letting it dissolve in a glorious blend of cocoa and butter.

She was *happy*...no, *delighted* everyone she knew was

here. She certainly didn't actually wish to be home alone on New Year's Eve watching that stupid ball drop and all those idiotic screaming people yelling as if it was actually a *good* night....

Hang on. Regroup. Nothing productive could come of her mind descending into negativity. That would lead to misery and depression and then she'd have to create an alternate world just to survive. And then she'd get dizzy and confused, try to eat a fork and end up dancing with a pillar. Then everyone would nod sagely, as if they'd all been right in predicting her complete mental breakdown after the Incident.

More chocolate needed.

Cassie took the largest piece of fudge, jammed it against the next biggest piece and shoved the whole thing in her mouth. *Close eyes. Absorb chocolate.* She was idolized by men. Worshiped by young girls. Inundated with rich clients all paying their bills ahead of time. A sexy diva with a killer tan. Her strappy sandals might be wildly inappropriate for the frigid December weather and snow on the ground, but they were perfect for showing off tanned feet. And they perfectly complemented the narrow black skirt and off-white angora sweater she'd donned to set off her lusciously golden skin. The entire ensemble also had been selected to make herself look sophisticated and classy. Like a woman to be reckoned with...not a woman who had just returned from a solitary honeymoon.

Yes, indeed. She was recovered and she was a dynamic, sexy single woman.... Ah. She felt better now.

Cassie opened her eyes and managed to smile calmly at her friend. "Is this a new recipe? It's amazing."

"As it should be. I'd have no right to call my chocolate shop Blissful Heaven if my creations weren't heavenly." Leo picked up a selection with shredded walnuts in it. "Try this one."

"One is good for me now." No need to admit she'd already eaten three. Sometimes it was better to deny reality, especially if it might make her question her inner fortitude. "I'm not in need. Yet. Do you have a pocket or something? I'm sure I'll need it later."

Later. Like when she ran into that miserable ex-fiancé who had nearly destroyed her life.... No. Be positive. Hmm...she'd need the chocolate later when she ran into the man to whom she owed all sorts of thanks for sparing her from making a horrible mistake....

Nope. Couldn't think altruistic thoughts about her ex-fiancé just yet. For now she'd just imagine him with his head chopped off and all would be good.

Leo wrapped the treat in a tissue and slid it into her purse. "For a stress management consultant with a Ph.D. in psychology, you're awfully uncreative when it comes to managing your own anxiety."

"So chocolate works best for me. Why is that uncreative?"

"It's just that you have about a zillion options in your arsenal when you're helping clients. I find it interesting that chocolate is the only thing that helps *you*."

"Maybe I'm just really dialed into myself. Self-aware." Brilliant, also. And gorgeous and sexy and...

"Or maybe you're just a chocoholic and you use stress as an excuse."

"Entirely possible." Cassie wiped her fingers with a napkin, then tossed it in the trash. "Besides, I'm not stressed. It's just the cold weather that's getting to me. Single digit weather and snowdrifts are a bit harsh after the sunny Bahamas."

"I thought you had bad weather?"

"No, why?" It had been gorgeous blue sky and bright yellow sun. Perfect weather to lure all those honeymooning couples out on the beach every day, cuddling and cooing. And those damn voodoo dolls Cassie had bought in that alley had done absolutely nothing to torture those imbecilic happy couples. Not that she'd really wanted to interfere with their blissful euphoria. It had merely been a scientific experiment designed to help her become an even better stress management consultant. If she'd managed to induce a tear or two from one of those asinine brides...well, all the better. No! She meant she would have gone over and *apologized*, not relished their suffering. Yeesh!

"You didn't spend your entire three weeks indoors, pining in misery for the wedding that didn't happen?"

Cassie stiffened. As if she'd spend a day weeping over that adulterous snake. "I was out in the sun the whole time. Why?"

"Huh."

"Huh, what?"

"How come you aren't tanned?"

"What? I'm so tanned."

Leo raised a blond eyebrow skeptically. "Are you?"

She'd left the Bahamas only this morning. Surely her tan couldn't have faded already? It was her proof to the world that she was psychologically stable. Recovered. How could anyone with a ravishing tan be anything but an emotional rock?

Okay, so it was a tenuous relationship at best, but it was all she had to work with. Cassie unfastened her gold watch and held out her wrist. "See? Tan line." *Phew.*

Leo squinted and lifted Cassie's wrist up close. "Oh,

yeah. I can see a faint mark. If I squint and pretend I'm on hallucinogenic drugs."

"Funny." Just what she needed right now: a sarcastic friend pretending not to notice her drop-dead-gorgeous tan. If Cassie wasn't so self-confident and stable, she might actually believe that Leo couldn't tell she was tan. And then she'd crumble into a sniveling lump because…

No! She'd promised herself there would be no thinking about cheating ex-fiancé's tonight. Who wanted a fiancé, anyway? Certainly not her. Nope. She was a movin' and shakin' kind of gal who was soon going to be inundated with requests to dance from all the gorgeous rich men at this very fancy affair.

Okay, so it was a school gym. So what? It was still decorated with streamers and balloons. And the DJ was really quite good. At any moment one of those gyrating teenagers or jitterbugging senior citizens was going to realize she was available and come racing across the floor to buy her a drink. Okay, fine. So they'd offer to get her a Coke. It was dark, crowded and loud; therefore, it was a party and the place to be.

Oh, yeah. She could shake with the best of them. Bump and grind. She elbowed Leo. "I think that kid over there wants to ask me to dance." She nodded toward a skinny redhead with braces. "He's pointing at me."

"He was supposed to be one of the ushers at your wedding. He's pointing you out so everyone will notice you're here."

"Oh." Well. Wasn't that a kicker? No, that was fine. *Let them stare.* Cassie lifted her chin. They'd see she was a total diva. "I'm Teflon."

Leo lifted her eyebrow. "Pardon?"

"I'm Teflon. No comments are going to get to me."

"Is that one of the lines you feed your strung-out clients?"

"It works."

"How? By deluding yourself?"

"Delusions can be very effective in managing tension," Cassie said.

"Doesn't mean they're a good thing. Just ask any ex-junkie who tried to make love to a motorcycle."

"What are you talking about?"

Leo grinned. "I have a date with a biker tomorrow night. Gotta get in the mind-set."

"Sometimes you frighten me."

"And you scare me all the time. Obviously, that's why we're best buds. A perfect match." Leo peered out into the crowd, no doubt searching for a man with whom she could bring in the New Year, if the low cut of her sweater and the waggle of her hips was any indication.

"So, any hot dates while I was gone?" Leo's sordid social life would be certain to distract Cassie from the fact that this dance was supposed to be her first appearance in town as Mrs. Drew Smothers and, instead, she was alone, bitter and barely tan. Or that's how she probably looked to outsiders. Internally, she was overwhelmed with a genuine appreciation for the wonder that was her life.

"Oh, you know. Plenty of dates. None of them hot enough to satisfy a bitter divorced woman like myself." Leo straightened her spine and narrowed her gaze on a distant corner. "But now that you're single, you can double-date with me as we conquer the world of single men."

Cassie's smile faltered. "I've been single for three

weeks. After four years of being in a relationship, I'm not ready to date. Especially a biker."

"I didn't invite you on that date. I'm keeping him for myself." Leo peered at her. "I do, however, think you should get out there again."

"You're wrong." What a ridiculous thing to say.

"Am I?"

"Absolutely." Cassie folded her arms across her chest. "I don't need a man."

"You're afraid."

"I am *not* afraid."

Burned by having her heart puréed by the lecherous viper she had loved for four years and almost married? Maybe...

Afraid of trusting her judgment when it came to men? Only when it came to those who were actually breathing.

Certain she was going to end up a wobbly spinster who had conversations with major appliances on a regular basis because she had no one else to talk to? Entirely possible.

But afraid of dating? Not a chance.

"Ah-hah!" Leo grabbed Cassie's arm. "I see two hot guys I don't know. Let's go introduce ourselves."

"Guys?" As Leo led her around the edge of the dance floor, Cassie's chest tightened and her breath began wheezing in her lungs. She leaned back and tried to twist her arm out of Leo's grasp. "Let go of me."

"No." Leo tightened her grip on Cassie's arm. "You look like an idiot fighting me. Smile and look sexy."

"I hate you," Cassie managed to whisper, just before Leo stopped in the darkened corner where two men—wearing suits and sporting broad shoulders and narrow waists—were standing.

"Hi, I'm Leo."

Both men nodded and grunted something, but Cassie couldn't hear them over the pounding music and surrounding babble of neighboring party-goers. All she could do was stare at the man on the right. Taller than his friend by at least a family pack of Oreos, his hair was dark, his eyes coal-black, and the shadow of a day's whiskers framed his jaw.

And amazingly enough, he wasn't gawking at Leo, drooling for one of her smiles. He was inspecting Cassie in the way a *man* inspected a *woman*. Whew. No one had looked at her like that in years.

It must be her single status. She was subconsciously sending out mating vibes that only the sexiest and most worthy men would respond to. Cassie phero-mones combined with her gorgeous tan were obvi-ously a powerful combination. See? She didn't need to be married. This dating thing would be a breeze.

"We're going to go dance. See you in a little bit," Leo said, slipping her arm through the elbow of the other man.

"What?" Cassie squawked. *Nice, Cassie.* Sound a lit-tle more panicked about being left alone with the sexi-est man she'd noticed in years. Decades even.

So much for the facade of being suave, sophisticated and mentally sound.

Leo was already gone, whirling into the crowd with her latest conquest in tow.

Cassie cleared her throat and tried to think of what a single woman was supposed to say to a devastatingly handsome man at a New Year's Eve celebration. For the last four years, while she'd been happily taken, she could rattle off brilliantly engaging conversation with anyone. But now that she was single, it was as if her brain had abandoned her to go play Ping Pong and her tongue had gone off to watch the match.

"I'm Ty." Obviously not suffering from the same affliction as she was, Ty held out his hand and sounded as if he were in complete control of all his faculties.

"Hi." She shook his hand, startled by the firmness of his grasp. Like a steel vise under the flesh, a clamp that could bind her and trap her in all sorts of wonderfully interesting ways....

"And your name is?" Ty prompted.

"Oh. Right. It's..." Why had she let Leo take the fudge with her? "My name...it's...Cassie." Phew. The tough part out of the way.

Ty nodded.

She smiled.

The music blared.

Wow, was she a dazzling conversationalist or what? Scintillating. It was astonishing she'd had only the one marriage proposal.

"So, um..."

He took his eyes off the dance floor. "Yes?"

"I..." *Where was her brain?* "Nice suit."

"Came straight from work."

"Work? But it's..." She glanced at the watch that hid the evidence of her marvelously bronzed skin. Maybe she should switch it to her other wrist. "It's almost eleven o'clock on a New Year's Eve. What do you do?"

"Financial consultant."

"Oh." *Think of an interesting response.* "I had a piggy bank when I was a kid."

He cocked an amused eyebrow. "Was it pink?"

"Yes. I named her Willemina and..." Cassie stopped. "Oh, wait. You were making fun of me."

"Not at all. I had a piggy bank of the Pillsbury

Doughboy. He's my inspiration." But Ty was grinning now, his eyes twinkling.

Cassie grimaced. "Okay, so it wasn't the smoothest pickup line."

"You were trying to pick me up?" He shot her a wary glance.

"Pick you up..." Why hadn't she left her tongue at home tonight? First thing Monday morning, she was having it surgically removed. "No, I meant...um, it was...casual conversation..."

Ty grunted and she felt his eyes on her again. "Where'd you get the tan?"

Cassie couldn't stop the swell of warmth that surged through her veins. He'd noticed her sun-kissed skin. Even Leo hadn't noticed. *Grab this man and run.*

Ack! *Shut up, hormones.* She wasn't interested in a man. She was single and damn happy about it. "I just got back from the Bahamas. My honeymoon."

Her honeymoon? Portraying herself as married to an incredibly handsome man who was perceptive enough to notice her tan? Just plain stupid. Definite choke under pressure. Or it would be if she'd been trying to impress him. Which she wasn't.

Ty's gaze flicked to her left hand, one eyebrow quirking when he spotted her bare finger.

Self-consciously, Cassie slid her hand out of view. "Um. It wasn't actually my honeymoon. I mean, it was supposed to be my honeymoon. I went alone."

Both of his luxuriously dark eyebrows were raised now and he wasn't looking at her tan anymore. He was staring into her eyes, as if he really wanted to know what secrets she was hiding.

Or she was hallucinating from too much chocolate.

"How'd you end up going on your honeymoon alone? Sounds like an interesting story."

"You must be new in town."

He blinked, probably startled by the change in subject. "Actually, I've lived here for six months," he said. "Why?"

"Are you a hermit? It's pretty much the only way you could have lived here and not heard about my amazing wedding or lack thereof."

"That juicy, huh?"

"In comparison to the number of other interesting things that happen in this town during December, yes." She lifted her brow. "So? Hermit?"

He glanced at her. "I work."

"You mean, you never get out of the house to socialize so you have no idea what goes on in this town and you have no friends?" Amazing! One person in town with whom her reputation was intact! A glorious feeling!

He narrowed his eyes, obviously not appreciating her free therapy. "So? What happened with your wedding?" He touched her arm suddenly. "Unless you don't want to talk about it. I didn't mean to pry."

Oh, she was definitely going to melt. A seriously hot guy who respected her privacy. What more could a woman ask for?

Maybe being single wouldn't be so bad, after all.

"Cassie? Is that you?" The voice of her ex-fiancé shattered her fantasy like a rock through a stained glass window.

I don't hear you.

"Cassie?"

Crud. She'd heard that. *Go away.*

But the whine of his voice grew closer and she knew

the infectious poison wasn't going to be deflected. He was coming. She slapped her hand against the wall and bent over, bracing herself as her stomach congealed into a sodden lump, dropped to her toes and began to ooze out the soles of her feet.

What a fine time to discover she wasn't actually ready to face Drew yet. It would have been exponentially more convenient to have that realization *before* she'd vomited all over his feet. And Ty's feet. Not that she was actually going to vomit. She was way too emotionally together to do something pathetic like that.

She hoped.

Note to self: sometimes delusions weren't a good thing. Like thinking she could fly. Imagine if she thought she could fly, and jumped off the Empire State Building. A clear example of when a delusion could be a bad thing.

Or imagine attending a dance where your ex-fiancé would be. Imagine thinking you were prepared to face him, only to learn that no, you actually weren't.

A great little nugget she'd be sure to incorporate into her future de-stressing strategies.

See? Something good could come of every situation. Was she a plucky survivor or what?

"Are you okay?" Ty's amused expression had morphed into one of endearingly genuine concern. Or it would have been endearing if she wasn't feeling so ill. What was up with the chocolate? It obviously wasn't working exceptionally well at the moment. He touched her shoulder, his hand warm and reassuring through the soft angora. "You don't look so hot."

"Thanks. It's every girl's dream to be told she doesn't look hot." Deep breaths. Deep breaths.

Ty's cheeks turned a faint red, or at least she thought

they did. It was hard to tell in the dim light with her eyes getting all foggy and the room starting to spin. "I didn't mean it like you didn't look good. You do look good. Pretty. Not that I noticed. I just meant you look like you don't feel well."

She would have patted his arm in consolation, if she weren't clinging to the wall for dear life. "Just a touch of indigestion. I'm fine. Really."

"Cassie! It is you." An unwelcome hand latched on to her arm. "I didn't realize you were back."

She saw Ty's eyes flick over her shoulder, and she knew this was her moment. All eyes in the room would be surreptitiously aimed in their direction, hoping for a scandal, a scene...anything to gossip about.

She could spin around, slam her knee into Drew's crotch and then saunter off as if she were a total diva. Or she could remember that some people in the room were future clients and might not be all that impressed with a stress management consultant perpetrating violent acts on the weaker sex.

Refusing to contemplate the irony that her emergency stash of chocolate was in Leo's purse on the dance floor, much too far away to be of any use whatsoever, Cassie took a deep breath and lifted her chin.

Then she plastered a brilliant smile on her face and turned to face her ex-fiancé, Drew Smothers. "Hi, Drew."

There he was, in his blond glory, his suit that... hmmm...didn't seem to fit nearly as well as Ty's did. And he was wonderfully pale, a victim of December in Gardenbloom.

"Didn't you take our tickets?" he asked.

She frowned. "Yes."

"Bad weather?"

Bastard. Cassie peeled off her watch and stuck out her wrist. "Any more questions?"

"Oh. I see. Your skin never did take to the sun well, did it?"

"Ty noticed my tan."

"Ty?" Drew echoed blankly.

Sweet, wonderful Ty settled his left arm around her waist, then extended his right hand toward Drew. "Ty Parker. Nice to meet you."

Good God. Not only was Ty a total hottie, but he was perceptive, too. Unbelievable.

Drew barely managed a handshake, gawking at Cassie. "He's...he's with you? But...I assumed you'd be alone."

"She's not." Ty wrapped his arm tighter around Cassie's waist, his thumb rubbing almost absently against her hip. And he smelled damn good. Tantalizingly delicious. Like spicy woods. Raw and masculine, yet refined and tender. She inhaled deeply, trying desperately not to be obvious as she prepared to pass out from olfactory bliss.

Maybe she'd add that to her list of de-stressors. Soothing scents...which would obviously differ from person to person.

She knew what worked for her. Maybe she could bottle Ty and keep him on her dresser.

Or by her bed.

Or better yet, in her bed.

"Cassie's with me," Ty said possessively, sending chills down her spine.

He swung his arm around her shoulder and hauled her up against his side. The man was like a rock and she fit perfectly under his arm. The heat from his body was so intense that she felt her insides begin to bubble and simmer. "You haven't introduced yourself, yet," Ty added. "Always like to meet the folks from my girl-friend's life."

His girlfriend?

Drew's face was hard, his lips a thin line. "I'm Drew."

"Drew who?" Ty began twirling his fingers in the soft tendrils of hair hanging beside Cassie's neck, an in-timate action that wasn't missed by Drew. Or by her. She felt as if her knees were going to buckle. Never had Drew's touch made her feel like all her bones had melted. Never had anyone's touch made her feel like this. Like...like wow.

Drew sighed impatiently. "I'm *Drew*."

Ty glanced blankly at Cassie. "Should I know who he is?"

Hide the grin, Cassie.

Drew's cheeks were turning an interesting shade of purple, making his head look sort of like a gigantic red grape. "I'm Drew Smothers. The man she was sup-posed to marry three weeks ago."

Ty didn't even react. "Oh. Well, nice to meet you."

Okay, there was a new definition of the word "hero" in her dictionary. It was Ty. Not only had he recog-nized a maiden in distress, but he'd also vaulted onto his white steed to rescue her. Not that she needed res-cuing, but she certainly wasn't going to turn down the offer.

She definitely owed him a free de-stressing session or two.

Or maybe she'd just sign over her entire savings to him.

Or maybe she'd pay with her body.

Yeah, right. As if she could even be that wanton. That wasn't her nature, even for a modern-day knight.

Drew lowered his voice and scowled at Cassie as if Ty, leaning over her shoulder, wouldn't be able to hear him. "How could you go to another man already? Didn't I mean anything to you? After four years together, you can just forget about us?"

"Forget? About us?" She was so stunned, she couldn't string more than two words together at a time. "How can...but you...with *her*..."

"It was a mistake. A one-time thing. Prewedding jitters. I still love you. It'll never happen again."

The absurdity of his claim released the dam and the words came tumbling free. "Prewedding jitters is sitting up all night unable to sleep, wondering if you're doing the right thing. Prewedding jitters is calling up your fiancée to remind yourself of all the things you love about her. Prewedding jitters is *not* having sex with another woman the night before your wedding!"

She heard Ty suck in his breath and make a sound as if he was choking.

Okay, so he hadn't known about the Incident. He did now.

Drew grabbed her hand, ignoring her when she tried to peel his fingers off hers. "Cassie! I love you! I'm not going to give up fighting for you."

Cassie yanked her hand free, trembling with rage. "Get away from me."

"Not until you give me another chance." The lascivious jerk had a glint of cockiness in his eyes as if he knew she'd fall victim to his carefully orchestrated plea, as she always had in the past whenever he'd irritated her.

But this time was different.

It wasn't about being annoyed.

This was about the essence of her soul.

Of her pride in being a woman.

"Cassie, just give me a chance. Lunch tomorrow. We'll start over. I'll prove you can trust me again."

Ignoring Drew, she turned to face Ty. His eyes were too dark to read in the dim light. He was like a mysterious black hole that could hold danger, intrigue, friendship, passion.... She had no idea.

It was a risk she had to take.

With Drew's incessant blathering rattling in her ears, she threw her arms around Ty and linked her hands behind his neck. She was uncomfortably aware of the look of surprise on his face, but she wouldn't stop. Not with Drew standing there.

She pulled Ty toward her and kissed him. Hard. With all the passion of someone who wanted to prove she was stronger than she really was, and who was totally undone by the handsomeness of the man she was kissing.

2

TY FELT AS IF HIS WORLD was exploding. He'd seen the kiss coming and been ready for it.

Or so he'd thought.

He hadn't been prepared for his blood to crash through his veins like a tidal wave trying to burst out of his body. He hadn't been ready for the fire that was instantly ignited down south, for his hands to snap around her, anchoring her against him while he returned her kiss with a fervor more appropriate for a clandestine affair between lovers than a kiss engaged in only to make her ex-fiancé feel like the bastard he was.

Ty couldn't stop himself from spreading his hands across Cassie's back, feeling her shoulder blades move under his fingers as she tightened her grip on him, pressing herself closer. And when the delicate murmur of pleasure echoed from her throat, Ty couldn't stop himself from responding with his own masculine growl of possession and passion.

He could feel Cassie's breasts flattened against his chest through his suit jacket and starched shirt, felt his own body rise in response. And when the kiss became intimate in a way that an outsider could never see, his response was for her alone, for only the two of them. Only they knew he could feel the smooth surface of her teeth with his tongue and that she was responding with her own exploration, each touch sending the fire in his body escalating to new heights.

"He's gone." Leo's amused voice broke through his fog.

Their lips froze, locked in the kiss like a pair of teenagers wearing braces.

"I said, Drew is gone." Leo's voice was louder now and even more amused.

Finally, Ty broke the kiss, but didn't let go of Cassie. She kept her hands around his neck, staring at him with a look of startled awe. "I know," he said.

Cassie blinked and finally appeared to realize what she was doing. Color rushed into her cheeks, turning them red through the bronzed tint of her skin, and she released him so quickly it was as if she'd been burned. Which was exactly how he felt. With regret, he let his hands slide off her soft sweater as she stepped away from him.

Leo moved into his line of vision, lowering her voice to a conspiratorial whisper. "That looked like one hot kiss."

Cassie's cheeks turned even redder, though he wouldn't have thought that was possible. "Um...Drew was being a jerk, so I, um, you know... I couldn't let him...and Ty was being so nice...and Drew...idiot...so I guess I had to do something...."

How could a woman capable of delivering a kiss like that be so genuinely embarrassed and cute afterward? There had been nothing "cute" about that kiss, yet now he wanted to wrap his arms around her and snuggle up with her to watch a movie in companionable intimacy. And then he'd take her to bed for some of that lovin'.

Hell, what was he thinking? He had no business letting his mind wander in that forbidden direction.

Cassie turned toward him, her eyebrows puckered in mortification. "Um, Ty, I'm really sorry about that."

"No need to apologize." No need at all. He'd take that kiss with him to his grave.

"No, really. I'm not the type to molest men I don't know."

"Or even men she does know," Leo chimed in.

Cassie nodded. "Right. I don't attack men. I swear." She pressed her thumb and index finger into her forehead and shook her head. "I'm so embarrassed."

Ty chuckled. "Trust me, any woman who can kiss like that has no reason to be embarrassed."

She furrowed her eyebrows and pursed her lips, as if she wasn't sure whether he was serious. Surely she'd gotten compliments before. No man could be the recipient of a kiss like that and not fall at her feet.

A strange pain in his gut surprised him. Was he actually bothered by the thought of her kissing other men as she'd just kissed him? He'd have to get over that and fast. Time to depart and get away from her influence.

There were certain things he didn't want to know about himself, and his reaction to Cassie was one of them. Engaged men simply didn't have those kinds of reactions to other women. Entirely unacceptable, regardless of whether the love between himself and his fiancée extended beyond friendship or not.

When he'd asked Alexis to marry him, he'd committed to her, and that's how it was going to stay. So what if they both knew their relationship was based on friendship, not romantic love? When her parents had died, he'd vowed to take care of her, and he would. Committing to a marriage that had no hope of romantic love wasn't a sacrifice. He'd never been in love in his life, so it wasn't as if he was forgoing that sort of opportunity.

Or at least, he hadn't thought so until Cassie's kiss created a possibility that loomed most unwelcome.

"I have to go," Ty said. "Nice to meet you, Cassie."

He left the two women staring after him, Leo looking utterly delighted and entertained and Cassie still looking as if she wanted to crawl beneath one of the tables and hide under the paper tablecloth until everyone was gone. He wanted to stay to reassure her that she had nothing to be embarrassed about....

Which was why he had to leave.

Now.

And consider buying a house in a different town.

Or a different state.

Or better yet, a different country.

He had a bad feeling that even Australia wouldn't be far enough to make him forget about Cassie.

CASSIE WATCHED TY disappear through the raucous crowd, her cheeks still roasting.

"Wow. Was that kiss as good as it looked?" Leo folded her arms across her chest and wiggled her eyebrows.

"Depends." It was absolutely astonishing that Cassie was able to speak coherently. She was truly gifted in her ability to don an exterior that hid the fact that her insides had melted. "How good did it look?"

"Like we should've called the fire department."

Cassie plopped down on a folding chair and propped her chin on her hands. "The fire department would've been impotent."

Leo sat down across from her and whistled. "That hot, huh?"

"If we hadn't been in a roomful of people, I think it's very possible I would have thrown him down and torn off that gorgeous suit." Cassie sighed and leaned on the table. Her body was still tingling where Ty's hands had held her, and his scent seemed to have settled in the fibers of her sweater. It was almost as blissfully heavenly as Leo's chocolate concoctions. Cassie had never felt like this with Drew.

Drew. Now, why did she have to go and ruin a perfectly good moment by thinking of *him?* Very annoying.

"*That* would have been something, to see you throw Ty on the table and rip his clothes off," Leo said. "Speaking of worthy visions, Drew stormed out the emergency exit, with a veritable billow of smoke coming out his ears."

As the heat began to subside in Cassie's body, sense began returning to her brain. An unwelcome phenomenon from both angles. "Good God, Leo. I attacked him."

"Yes, you did. Quite brilliant, really."

"No, Leo, it's a bad thing. I made a complete fool of myself in front of the entire town."

Leo snorted. "Nonsense. At least half the town isn't here."

Like that made a difference. Cassie moaned and dropped her head to her arms, trying to bury her face in the table. "I'm going back to the Bahamas."

"Don't be ridiculous. The man loved it. You could see it all over his face."

Cassie lifted her head off the table. "Really?"

"Yep. Maybe he could be your rebound man. Have a

wild fling with him that restores your faith in yourself as a sexual dynamo when it comes to men."

"I'm not a sexual dynamo." A sexual flat tire was a more accurate description.

"I bet Ty would say you were."

"I doubt it." But a flutter of hope danced in Cassie's belly at the thought. Wouldn't *that* be interesting? As if it would happen. "Besides, I'm not ready for a relationship."

"Because Drew burned you."

"Don't be ridiculous. I just want to be single. I'm not upset about Drew at all."

Leo raised her eyebrow and Cassie lifted her chin. As if she'd ever let Drew win. "I could, however, use a little chocolate."

Leo hopped to her feet. "Nothing like chocolate to solve a woman's problems. After that display, I'm sure you're in need of some therapy."

"It's going to take the entire dessert table." And then some. Drew and a wanton display of impropriety all in the same evening? Not a good start to her life as a single woman.

Not a good start at all.

IT HAD BEEN LONG ENOUGH. Eight days since she'd returned from her honeymoon unwed. Eight days since she'd sucked face with a hot guy in front of her ex-fiancé. Eight days for her tan to fade.

Time to get her business going again. With the wedding approaching and Drew trying to convince her to close up shop so she could play little wifey, she'd been too stressed...ahem...*busy* to spend much time drumming up new clients.

Didn't she look like the smart one now, refusing to

listen to Drew and give up her career? What kind of shape would she be in currently if she'd quit her job *and* had no husband? Oh, and the monstrous bill from the wedding that she'd footed because Drew had insisted that was the bride's responsibility. Mustn't forget about that souvenir from the Almost Biggest Mistake of Her Life.

Cassie tapped her fingers on the steering wheel as she peeled around a snowy corner in her trusty Subaru. Maybe Drew had been trying to bankrupt her before the wedding so she would be financially dependent on him.

Bastard.

Anyway, she was totally over that, had spent the week cleaning up her office, closing accounts with old clients and opening files with new ones.

So what if she'd totally forgotten she'd promised to start Malcolm Tyler Parker's treatment right after she got back from her honeymoon? She was on her way there now, wasn't she? What was a week, huh?

Okay, so it was unforgivable that she'd misplaced the file. Fine. She could admit it. Perhaps she'd been a wee bit unsettled by the last month. She was together now.

Cassie coasted to a stop at a red light and glanced at her watch. Ten minutes to seven. She'd been planning to show up at Mr. Parker's at exactly seven in the morning.

Her usual modus operandi for a new client.

Sure, he'd called her to set up a consultation, saying he was having trouble sleeping. That didn't mean he'd actually ever tell her what was really going on. That was why she'd developed her strategy with all her new clients.

Show up unannounced at a bad time to start therapy. The client was always super stressed, and she usually got a very good idea of what she was dealing with.

There was a reason why she'd been written up in the *New York Times* as an excellent stress therapist. She was brilliant. How could she feel bad about herself if she kept pumping herself up like this? She couldn't. Was she smart or what? It was a good thing she was so talented and got her own advice for free, or she'd be an emotional mess. And she *wasn't* an emotional mess, if anyone was asking.

Cassie drummed her fingers impatiently on the dashboard, waiting for the light to change.

What if her new client had been at the dance and seen her display? It was bad enough she'd shown up at the event dateless, but making out with some stranger in front of everyone? Imagine the damage that could do to her professional reputation...unless she could figure out a way to call it research. Hmm...

Then again, was heavy-duty lip action with a really gorgeous guy so bad? No doubt everyone was talking about how Drew had stormed out and how Cassie was totally together and emotionally magnificent after such heartbreak.

It wasn't as if anyone at the dance knew how close she'd actually come to vomiting all over Drew. Perhaps all was not lost...assuming she decided being known as a roving temptress was better than being known as "the woman who had a nervous breakdown and never recovered." She could just imagine when she was ninety-two and doddering about town, people pointing to her and saying, "She had such a promising future once and now she just sits home alone picking lint out of her carpet. What a shame. What a shame."

Instead, she'd be sauntering down the street at ninety-two with a horde of eager young bucks hoping to get a chance with the town's sexual dynamo trailing after her.

A ninety-two-year-old prostitute. Somehow, that just didn't have quite the ring she was looking for.

No matter. She'd just avoid men in every capacity and life would be good. Perhaps she should go back to the Bahamas and learn how to run from the giant bugs. Probably be less stressful than sorting out the oh-so-fabulous changes in her life.

Cassie whacked her forehead as she turned right onto Ridgeway Road. What was she thinking? She wasn't stressed. She was fine. Fabulous. Wunderbar.

Perfectly capable of normal everyday things, like noticing what a nice neighborhood she'd just turned into. She frowned. Actually, it was really nice. Like, her dream neighborhood. Old, charming and classically New England. Houses with big wraparound porches, exuding character and personality.

Then she saw her destination: 153 Ridgeway Road.

That was it. She was officially in love with this house.

It was her dream home. Six dormers, three brick chimneys, huge windows. How could she possibly have lived in this town for her entire life and never known of the house? It should have called to her and forced her to find it.

Not that she could have afforded it, but still, she could have at least tried to find the money. Maybe she could have sold her body to wealthy old men for a few nights...yeah, right. No way could she sacrifice her body to dirty old men, no matter how nice the house was. The guy from the New Year's Eve dance was another matter entirely....

Ack! What was she thinking?

Ty had been a mistake, albeit a fun one given Drew's reaction, but a lapse in judgment nonetheless. He was still a man and, as such, didn't deserve to be thought of fondly. Starting now, men didn't exist except as target practice when she was driving her car. Oh, and as clients and, therefore, as a way to fill her bank account.

And people thought she was bitter. Hah!

She was fine and ready to work, dammit. So she pulled into the driveway of her dream house and shut off the ignition.

She pushed her car door open with her foot, testing the driveway for traction.

Ice hidden beneath a dusting of snow.

Looked friendly. Treacherous beneath the surface. Just like a man.

But she meant that in the most complimentary way possible, because she really *didn't* have baggage that was going to destine her to become an ill-tempered, unwanted old lady who chased little children with her cane just to hear them scream.

Not that she was paranoid that she'd never have another chance to get married again. *That* was a ridiculous notion. The last thing she wanted to do was date another man, let alone get married. The fact that she was starting over in the dating arena at age twenty-seven? *No problem.* She couldn't have planned her life better if she'd tried. Everything was *perfect.*

She planted other foot solidly on the ground, grabbed her personal digital assistant that was oh-so-handy for downloading straight into her computer, straightened her suit, dug her heels into the snow for traction and prepared herself to march up to the door of her new client and change his life.

Hmm...maybe she should get a dog. Drew had always been antidog, but he was gone now, wasn't he? If she got a dog, at least there would be one male who would share only her bed at night. Floppy ears, thick fur, four legs and a tail now topped her list of desired attributes in a man. Wouldn't that be entertaining, if she started asking her dates to drop their pants so she could inspect for a tail?

See? There was humor in her miserable life.

Dammit. She'd used that word again: *miserable.* If she kept doing so, someone was bound to think she actually felt that way. She must eradicate it from her vocabulary, effective immediately.

She watched her breath puff out in white clouds as she hurried up the steps, carefully balancing her weight so her feet didn't slip out from under her. *Think about the client.* Right. She could do this. Concentrating was no problem. She was a highly sought after professional genius, right? Of course right. She was never, ever wrong.

Okay...so find the significance of the icy steps.... Wow. It was like her brain was in a deep freeze. *Come on, Cassie! Think! No, don't panic that you've lost your talent. Close your eyes. Take deep breaths. Relax the muscles. Think about the client. Icy steps. Client. Stress.*

Got it! Obviously, Malcolm Tyler Parker was too busy to put sand on his steps. Very interesting.

Cassie pulled out her PDA and jotted down the information. The man couldn't sleep and didn't take care of his property. Good to know. She entered the information in the "failure to perform basic home maintenance" column and proceeded to the door.

Hopefully, her new client would be an easy fix.

She wasn't sure she was up to a monstrous challenge with a recalcitrant client, not with her soul still splattered on the pavement and trampled by a herd of rampaging cattle.

Scratch that.

She was fine.

Her soul was intact.

Her ego...maybe a little frayed around the edges. Nothing that a quick hem job couldn't fix. If only she knew how to sew...

She forced herself to take a leisurely moment to admire the old horseshoe that had been converted into a door knocker, then banged on the door.

One minute after seven. Perfect timing.

No one came to the door.

She knocked again.

Still no one.

Cassie frowned. Surely he hadn't left already? She clicked on "work schedule" to double-check her file. Yes, he'd told her he left for work shortly after seven. He should still be there. Her notes were never wrong.

She knocked again, harder, pretending it was Drew's head she was pounding against the wood. Ah, how soothing. Taking her own advice to identify her stresses and visualize resolution, however socially inappropriate or legally prohibited.

She was definitely a genius.

A door slammed inside the house and Cassie straightened. She patted her hair to make sure it was neat, checked her nylons for runs, clamped her teeth together so they wouldn't chatter from the cold, ignored her desire to rush home and put on flannel-lined blue jeans, fleece-lined boots and a wool sweater, and readied herself to face her new client.

With any luck, he would be extremely annoyed by the interruption and she could see what he was really like. She was on a roll now. The old Cassie was back. She should become an inspirational speaker on how to recover from emotional devastation. She was *that* amazing.

The unmistakable click of a lock being opened cued her to don a demure smile that would neither propel her new client into more stress nor dissipate stress that might already be present. Was she good or what?

The door opened and she forgot everything. "You're kidding."

"Cassie? What are you doing here?"

It was Ty.

From New Year's Eve.

The same Ty with whom she'd tongue-tangoed eight days ago.

This was *so* not turning out to be her month.

3

MALCOLM TYLER PARKER.

Ty.

Duh.

Was she an idiot or what? So blinded by his gallantry that she hadn't noted the possibility that "Ty" and "Malcolm Tyler" could be the same person.

Idiot. Idiot. Idiot.

"You're Malcolm Tyler Parker, aren't you?" As if she needed to ask.

He scowled. "How did you know my name? Or where to find me? I'm not in Information." His voice was cautious, his body blocking the doorway as if to keep her out of his house.

"You gave it to me." Sure sign of his stress. Didn't even recall hiring Halloway Consulting to save him. *There you go, Cassie. Think about work and not about how completely embarrassed you are to be standing here on his doorstep thinking about what his tongue feels like against yours.*

He raised an eyebrow and shifted in the doorway, then shifted again. Too tense to relax? He was in such need of her services. "I told you my name was Ty. Didn't give you my full name or my address."

"Sure you did. How else would I have gotten it?"

Ty frowned and, despite her best efforts, she couldn't help but notice that he looked quite sexy in his suit. In the light of day, it was apparent that Ty's eyes were not black. They were a deep brown and they were narrowed in…disgust? Irritation? Raging desire for her body?

And he smelled *so good*. It was the same scent that had embedded itself in her sweater on New Year's Eve…and hadn't left the fibers all day Sunday.

Not that she'd pressed the sweater to her face all day or slept with it under her pillow just so she could smell him….

Definitely not.

Cassie! What was she doing? Ty's enticing scent was clearly not what she should be concerned about. A much bigger issue was his stress. And how she was going to explain sexually assaulting him a week ago.

Damn. She *was* going to have to explain that one.

But he really did look good in the light of day, didn't he? He was the epitome of a wealthy businessman heading into New York City for work. A ridiculously sexy capitalist who undoubtedly had stolen many a woman away from her man.

Not that Cassie was attracted to him. She didn't go for the corporate type. Except for Drew, and that had worked out oh-so-well. She'd always fantasized about the down-home boy who'd sling the kids over his shoulder and take them to work with him. A man who'd come home during lunch to build a new tree house. But Ty, with his sleek suit and efficient haircut, was giving her second thoughts on that particular stance. Maybe it was because she had no trouble picturing him with a kid hanging from each arm and a cat clawing its way up his leg. Either she was ultraperceptive or it was the first sign of the gradual deterioration of her grip on reality.

Perhaps it was his slightly crooked tie that was softening his image. Hmm…the off-kilter tie was probably a sign of his stress. A man who took such obvious care with his appearance couldn't quite get the details right.

He needed her.

Ty's eyes narrowed and Cassie realized how thick and dark his eyelashes were. So sexy they nearly made her pass out…. Well, if she were the fainting type.

"Why are you here? It's not about New Year's Eve, is it? Because that didn't mean anything. It was to make Drew suffer because he's a jerk."

Oh, wow. He thought she was stalking him. *Super.* What an excellent first impression for a stress management therapist. *Hi, I'm your therapist. Let me suck on your tongue and then stalk you.*

No problem. She could handle this, right? Of course right. It wasn't as if she was an emotional wreck or anything from the wedding that never happened. She lifted her chin and smiled calmly, ignoring the swirling whirlpool in her belly. "Ty. Listen, I'm *not* here about the kiss."

"You aren't?" His eyebrows were raised in visible skepticism. "Then why are you here?"

"To do you. I mean to do your stress. I mean…" Oh, if only the porch would collapse under her right now and bury her beneath two-hundred-year-old boards. No such luck, as the house was apparently built much too solidly for her convenience. She cleared her throat. "Six weeks ago you hired me to de-stress you. I'm here. Therapy has begun."

He stared at her.

The man was like a mountain. An immovable mass of heaving masculinity. Oh, great. There went her hormones again, dancing 'round the campfire doing the "seduce me" dance. When she got home, she was going to have a little chat with them about behaving appropriately when in public places.

"I hired you." He did not sound convinced.

"Yes." She patted his shoulder, refusing to notice how hard his muscles were beneath her hand. Okay, fine, so she noticed a little. She was human, wasn't she? "Ty, that's a sure sign of stress, when you forget appointments."

He narrowed his eyes. "There's no way I forgot an appointment this morning."

Ah, he had her there. "Well, that's true. I was intending to surprise you this morning." From the deepening of the scowl on his face, he didn't appear to take kindly to surprises.

Probably still fretting that she was a stalker.

"Hang on." Cassie whipped out her handheld PDA, called up the original e-mail Ty had sent her to request her services, then turned the screen toward him. "Read."

He grabbed her hand to steady the screen, and Cassie's stomach did a little jump. What was her problem? He was a client, not some man put on this earth to give her thrills.

She didn't even like men anymore, remember? She certainly wasn't about to be attracted to one of them, even if she could still feel the heat from his hand infusing hers with...

"Huh." He released her hand suddenly, as if he'd just realized he was touching her. Jerk. Just because he thought she was a dangerous lunatic was no reason to treat her as if she had cooties. Or maybe he wanted her so badly he couldn't risk touching her. Good to know her imagination was still functioning.

"Now are you convinced you hired me?" Cassie flipped the screen toward herself and glanced at his e-mail. "You're having trouble sleeping, your fiancée insisted you contact me or else she wouldn't come home...."

Whoa! Fiancée! Cassie had forgotten about that! Since Ty was Malcolm Tyler Parker, her new client, he had a *fiancée*. That really sucked.

Or it would suck, if she were interested in dating ever again. Which she wasn't. So she didn't care. Professional interest only. The burning in her gut? The result of consuming only coffee for breakfast. Not the feeling of disappointment, misery, loneliness or anything stupid like that. "You're engaged?"

His lips tightened and his eyes darkened. For a long minute, he said nothing.

And then Cassie realized it was the Moment.

The moment where she learned whether all men were like Drew, cheating on their fiancées when they thought they wouldn't get caught.

Ty could lie to her.

His fiancée would never know.

Don't lie, Ty!

Not that Cassie cared. It wasn't as if she was looking for a hero or even believed they existed. And what if, by some fluke of nature, Ty actually was some moral, trustworthy guy who was loyal to his fiancée? Then he'd refuse to ravage Cassie's body and she wouldn't get him, anyway. And if he did offer to tear off her clothes and take her right there on the doorstep, then he'd be a cretin who cheated on his fiancée.

See how it worked? If he honored his commitment to his fiancée, then he'd be worth trusting, but then Cassie couldn't have him.

Not that she actually cared about *him*. It was just a hypothetical exercise in strategic thinking.

Ty finally nodded. "Yes, I'm engaged."

Relief and regret surged through her. He was worthy…and he was unavailable. A hero…belonging to someone else.

Or maybe he just didn't find her remotely attractive and he would have claimed a cockroach for a fiancée if it meant he didn't have to fend off another one of her attacks.

Not that she had self-esteem issues or anything like that.

She lifted her chin. "Well, that's great you have a fiancée. Fiancées are great." *Yes, as long as they don't rip your heart out of your chest and stomp all over it in a public forum.* "So, I guess then I'm supposed to de-stress you to save your engagement, huh? Make you tolerable to be around?"

For eight days she'd dreamed about this man…and now she had to ready him for another woman? If she failed and his fiancée ran away screaming, then he'd be available. If she succeeded, then he'd marry another woman.

Not that any of that mattered if the cockroach theory proved to be true.

And even if it didn't, she had a job to do.

Whoa. What was she thinking? She couldn't take this job.

He wasn't a client. He was a man whom she'd sexually assaulted only a week ago. And she could still taste him on her lips.

How could she ever maintain appropriate professionalism with this man, in this situation?

It was completely impossible.

She was tough, but she wasn't impenetrable.

Not to mention she was still mortally embarrassed about attacking him.

"Cassie? Are you all right?" His brows were furrowed and he actually looked sort of cute when he wasn't glaring at her and acting as if she was a psycho.

"I'm excellent."

"You sure?"

Damn him. He looked so concerned that she wanted to plop down on his couch and tell him all about her miserable month. No, *challenging* month. "Of course I'm sure."

He didn't look as if he believed her, and her belly became warm with appreciation. No doubt he was the kind of man who would take care of his woman. He might even realize when she needed a hug without her having to ask....

No. Don't think like that.

Think of the cockroach theory. "So...we have some work to do," she said.

"No, we don't."

Typical denial. "Because you aren't stressed or because you can't stand the sight of me after I molested you...?" Oh, super. How had that little gem found its way from her brain to her lips? She certainly hadn't given it a map.

An endearing smile tugged at the corner of his mouth. "I'm not stressed."

And what about the second part of my question? As if she'd ask. He'd ignored it and so would she.

"And the sight of you doesn't turn my stomach," he added, as if he could read her mind.

"Oh. Well. That's good.... I mean, it's good because it would be hard for us to work together if I made you nauseous." Brilliant. She was simply dazzling with her manipulation of the English language and her ability to turn a romantic phrase.

He grinned, no doubt amused by her ongoing effort to prove she was a complete dolt.

"The kiss has nothing to do with the fact I don't want your help," Ty said.

The kiss. The magical, earth-shattering, devastating kiss.

"I don't want your help because I don't need it. I thought I sent you another e-mail canceling the contract."

"Stress again. You think one thing, you do another, and all the while your subconscious knows you need help. It's typical." She flipped open the cover to her PDA again. "You don't mind if I take notes, do you?"

Ty grabbed the unit out of her hand. "I said I don't need help."

Excellent. A recalcitrant client. She was so not up for this. Recalcitrant, hot and a good kisser. Just what she needed.

Ty snapped the cover down. "For your information, I have a demanding job. That's it. I was busy, hadn't returned a couple calls to my fiancée and she got annoyed. So I sent the e-mail."

Ah-hah. He'd done a weird jerky thing with his eyes when he'd mentioned his job. Something wasn't right at the office. Cassie carved the note in her brain for recall after they'd parted ways and she could jot it down in her handheld device. Look at her: gifted with an attentive and sharp mind that honed in on stress-related signals even while she was in the throes of an emotional breakdown. Was she good or what? She'd always suspected there was a reason she hadn't tried to knock herself out with a coconut when she was in the Bahamas.

"So what if my job requires long hours? That doesn't mean I'm stressed," Ty added.

As if she was that brain-dead. The man was too transparent to escape her sleuthing and suspicious mind. Before Drew, she'd been naive and trusting. Today, she was a bitter, perceptive woman...or harlot, depending on one's point of view. Maybe having her world shattered by a cheating fiancé would make her a better stress management consultant. No longer would she be so willing to believe the good side her clients projected. A jaded realist, she would dig deeper than ever to find the true misery in her clients' lives. "And your fiancée? No worries about what might happen when she comes to town and finds you working such long hours?"

"Nope."

He didn't flinch there. Definitely no concerns about what his fiancée would think about his work schedule. But something was amiss. It was apparent from the way he shifted on the doorstep and looked at his watch....

Or maybe Cassie was making him late for a meeting.

Yikes. Why couldn't she tell the difference between his being late and his being deceptive? What had happened to her instincts? Left on the floor of Drew's bedroom on the night before their wedding, when she'd walked in...

Ahem.

Hadn't she banned herself from thinking about that night? *Focus on the present.* "So, I'll see you Friday night?"

He blinked. "Friday night?"

"Eight o'clock? Your place. I assume you don't get home early enough during the week to meet."

"I told you. I don't need your help."

Cassie shrugged, trying not to look into the depths of his dark eyes, wondering what it would feel like to have them roaming her body…. Hello. This was business. And he was engaged. Shut down the hormones.

Besides, hadn't she already decided she couldn't take him on as a client? There was simply too much baggage. And if she refused him as a client, then she wouldn't have to be near him. And that would be good because she certainly felt the same urge to attack him that had overwhelmed her on New Year's Eve, only this time she didn't have the excuse of wanting to destroy Drew's cockiness. Cassie was definitely going into post-traumatic stress disorder as a result of canceling the wedding. From conservative fiancée to sex-crazed fiend in a matter of weeks.

Not an entirely convenient transformation, given that the only two men in her life were a cheating ex-fiancé and a stressed-out hunk engaged to another woman. Not exactly appropriate outlets for her newly aroused fantasies. The solution? Retreat. "Fine. I won't help you."

He lifted an eyebrow. "Fine? Just like that?"

"Sure. Why not?"

"But…"

"But what?"

"Shouldn't you be more…"

"Tenacious?" she offered.

"Yes."

"Usually. Not today."

"Why not?"

"Not in the mood." To be more precise, she wasn't in

the mood to work with him, and she was taking any excuse to turn down the project. Not that she was too emotionally distraught to cope. It was a tactical ploy designed to lay the foundation for her future career. She held out her hand. "My PDA, please."

He passed it to her, his fingers brushing against her palm. Dammit! Why were her hormones going all weird every time he touched her? Unprofessional, inappropriate and pathetic. It was time to shape up. "Have a nice day."

She made it only to the curb before she started doubting her decision.

BY THE TIME CASSIE arrived at Blissful Heaven at nine o'clock that evening, Leo had already laid out a bountiful supply of lush strawberries. A pot of thick, gooey and sinfully delicious chocolate was heating on a burner. The smell of warm cocoa hit Cassie the moment she pushed open the door to the little shop.

Nirvana at last.

She inhaled deeply, waiting for the tension to leave her body.

It didn't.

She sniffed again, letting the divine scent spread through her being, seep into her lungs....

Again, no loosening of the tight tendons in her shoulders. What was up with that? Chocolate never failed her. She saved these emergency sessions for the moments of greatest need, and they always worked.

Of course, at the present moment, she was a wee bit more strung out than she'd been in the past. Like when she'd driven into a police car at a stoplight, or the time she'd accidentally set Drew's house on fire when he was on his way home with clients.... Hah! She'd forgotten about that. Must have been her prophetic subconscious knowing that someday he'd be deserving of having his kitchen turned into a pile of ashes on a very important day.

All well and good now, but at the time she had been more than a little distraught. A quick session at Leo's with the chocolate and Cassie had recovered enough to call Drew and admit she hadn't actually been killed in the fire. The jerk hadn't even been worried about her, a fact she probably should have paid more attention to.

Ah, the beauty of hindsight.

So, anyway, if the chocolate had worked for *that* very traumatic event, why wasn't it helping now, when things weren't nearly that bad? So she'd sucked face with some stranger who was engaged to another woman. So what if he was also her new client and she couldn't stop fantasizing about him? Those really weren't big deals, even if you threw in the minor issue of the wedding that never happened. Really. It wasn't any worse than, say, getting a bad haircut—especially if you got the haircut as your head was stuck through a guillotine and the blade was coming down, gleaming and shining, ready to lop off your head and—

"Cassie! You're here!" Leo popped up from behind the marble counter, her bleached-blond hair swept into a careful bun to keep stray strands from adding to the texture to her desserts. Her customers would no doubt rebel against finding strands in their succulent sweets, or at least the women would. Cassie suspected the men lived for the hope that such a blessing would befall them.

Men. A strange breed.

"What in the world is going on? You call an emergency chocolate relief session and then make me wait all day without any details! What's up with that?"

As if she was prepared to talk yet. She needed medicinal treatment first. Cassie grabbed the biggest strawberry and dunked it into the bubbling vat. She held it up, letting thick drops fall back into the pot with a rhythmic, soothing blurp. Ah...she felt better already just watching the chocolate dance. "It's Ty."

"Ty? The guy from New Year's Eve? You saw him again?"

Yes, I saw Sex God again. Smelled dreamy. No, she needed to regroup. Focus. "I'm supposed to de-stress him for his fiancée." Wow, that really sucked, saying "Ty" and "his fiancée" in the same sentence.

Cassie immediately plunked the chocolate-covered berry in her mouth.... Yikes! Hot!

"You're supposed to put those on the waxed paper to cool after you dunk them," Leo said dryly.

"Like I don't know that." The fact that she'd seared off the top layer of her tongue would be well worth it once the chocolate kicked in and soothed her stress....

"Wow. You're really in bad shape," Leo said.

"Hang on." Cassie held up a hand to stall Leo's inquisition while she assessed her body. One strawberry ingested, but she still didn't feel any better? Something was definitely wrong. Maybe the chocolate-fruit ratio had been off. Time to go full strength.

She picked up a spoon, dunked it into the simmering pot and scooped up a decadent portion.

"You must be seriously close to cracking up to assault your figure like that," Leo observed. "He's just a guy."

"My need for chocolate has absolutely nothing to do with him." Gah. How pathetic did Leo think she was?

Needing chocolate because of a man. Silliest thing she'd ever heard.

Cassie blew on the chocolate to cool it off. See? Her instincts were still working. She was capable of learning from her mistakes. Burn the tongue on hot chocolate once. Cool it off next time. Someone on the verge of losing her mind would be entirely incapable of such brilliance. "He thought I was stalking him when I first showed up."

"I wouldn't recommend the stalking thing."

Cassie raised an eyebrow. "Don't tell me you've been accused of stalking before?"

"I might have been a bit overzealous in my pursuit of men in my reckless youth, but we're discussing Ty. More specifically the fact that his engagement has sent you into a bout of depression so deep that it'll take my store's complete inventory to pull you out of it."

Cassie poured the entire contents of the spoon into her mouth and swallowed. "It's not that he's engaged."

Leo lifted her brows. "No?"

"It's that I nearly sampled his tonsils. How am I supposed to work with him?" Darn it. Still no relief. "Are you sure this is real chocolate?"

"I think he still wants to jump your bones. And I'm insulted you could even question the purity of my chocolate."

"Jump my bones?"

Leo grinned. "I told you. Biker date last night. I'm still in the mind-set."

Cassie folded her arms across her chest. "Well, Ty's engaged, so it doesn't matter if he wants me. Besides, the entire conversation is moot because I'm not going to take him on as a client and I'm never dating anyone ever again, anyway. And are you really positive it's not diet chocolate or something?"

"You're going to turn him down? Are you kidding? You have one kiss with the man and you can't cope with being in the same room with him? I'd have to go into isolation if I couldn't handle being in the presence of any man I'd kissed. And of course it's not diet."

But this kiss was different. It had been more than a kiss. It had been a connecting of their souls.

"Is Ty stressed?"

"No." *Liar! Liar! Liar!*

"Cassie…"

"Okay, fine. There's a distinct possibility he's stressed. So what?"

"So, you're going to abandon a person in need of your services? Don't you have any compassion?"

"I— He—" Where was her brain? Cassie was totally unable to fabricate even a weak excuse, let alone a viable one.

"Face it, Cassie. You called this chocolate relief session because you're feeling guilty for refusing to help him because of your own baggage."

"I have no baggage."

Leo rolled her eyes. "The wedding? Finding Drew naked with another woman? Him declaring his love for you at the dance? Throwing yourself at some hot guy? Your first kiss in four years with someone other than Drew? Broke from your own wedding?"

"Well, when you say it like *that*…" Forget the stupid red fruit. She needed chocolate straight up. Cassie scooped up another spoonful, blew on it, then dumped the entire contents in her mouth. Swirled it around. Twice. Swallowed.

Nothing!

No respite at all.

Was she building up an immunity?

Just what she needed: a resistance to chocolate. Not.

It certainly couldn't be that she was so tense that even her fail-safe stress reliever was rendered impotent. That would be unacceptable. Could she even imagine a stress-management consultant who was a complete basket case? Yes, that was definitely something that would add to her credentials.

Leo set her cellphone in Cassie's hand. "Call him."

Was she *insane?* "Ah... No." Cassie tossed the phone onto the counter.

"Ah, yes."

"No."

"Call him. Make a follow-up appointment. Five minutes with him and you both will have forgotten the kiss."

Not a chance of that.

"Wimp," Leo said.

"I'm not a wimp."

"Prove it."

Cassie frowned. Was Leo right? Had she dissolved into a helpless lump of pitiful femaleness just because her man had left her and the next man she'd kissed was engaged to someone else?

Nonsense.

She was too stable to be upset.

So, then, if she wasn't an emotional wreck, what reason did she have for turning down a perfectly good client who could pay his bills?

None.

Therefore, she would take the client and prove to everyone—most of all herself—that she was entirely in control of all her emotions.

She'd work with Ty on a professional level and forget about men as the opposite sex. And earn some money in the process. Because she was a rock. So there.

She pulled out her cellphone, pulled up Ty's home number and pressed Send.

Her heart was racing because she'd just ingested about one million times the lethal dose of sugar and caffeine, not because she was nervous about calling him. He was a client, for heaven's sake. Nothing special about him. Nothing special at all. Except, of course, his ability to rock her with the touch of his lips.

Not that she was thinking about it.

His answering machine picked up, as expected at nine o'clock on a Monday night. The man was probably still at work, poor sod. And to think she'd almost abandoned him. He *needed* her. In fact, wasn't that a good change? To have a man need her. It definitely put her in the position of power in the relationship.

Which was exactly where she deserved to be.

See? All was good.

With renewed energy and spirit, she said, "Ty, it's Cassie. I've changed my mind. You're in denial. You need my help. I'll be at your house a week from Friday. Eight in the evening. Be there."

She hung up before she could be tempted to blurt something completely contradictory, like she had no interest in helping him keep his fiancée and hell would freeze over before she'd embarrass herself by actually confronting him again. "Well. There we go. Done."

"A week from Friday? What's wrong with this Friday?"

"I'm in demand. A stress management consultant of my caliber would never have an opening that soon."

Leo nodded. "Excellent point. You have to play hard to get."

"Leo! I'm not trying to date him!"

"I didn't mention dating. You did."

"I did not."

Leo plucked one of the strawberries off the wax paper and held it up. "Cheers."

"Cheers." Cassie picked up a pristine strawberry and ate it without dipping it.

No longer could she deny the truth.

It was going to take a lot more than chocolate to get Ty's kiss out of her soul.

And she had eleven days to figure out how to do so.

Eleven days to figure out how to be in the same room with him without tearing off her clothes and hurling herself into his arms.

No problem.

4

ELEVEN DAYS LATER at precisely eight o'clock, Cassie pulled into Ty's driveway.... Oh, fine. It was half past eight and she'd driven by his road four times before finally turning onto it. But she was here, wasn't she? That was what mattered.

And it wasn't as if she'd spent the last eleven days thinking about him, either. She'd been working. Secured some other clients, had a few excellent counseling sessions and even got a new coffeemaker for the office. Certainly, she hadn't been thinking about Ty's kiss or his body or his fiancée or anything like that. Absolutely not. She was way too professional for that.

So she'd thought about him a little bit. She had to in order to work on his treatment plan, right? Of course right. Now she was here, ready to assess and add to her professional knowledge about him. And she wasn't thinking about any of those other issues at all. The fact she'd driven by his road four times before actually turning onto it? Merely a delay tactic to ensure she'd properly thought out her treatment plan prior to arrival.

Cassie slowed her car at the end of Ty's driveway. "Well, I'm here. I guess I should pull in, huh?"

No divine intervention appeared to encourage her to flee back to her own house and abandon her new client.

Right.

She could do this.

She pulled her Subaru into Ty's driveway and parked beside the garage. She'd just turned off her ignition when her car was flooded with lights from a car pulling in behind her.

Cretin. He was a half hour late for their appointment. Completely unprofessional.

No worries. She'd show him what their relationship was going to be like. All-business, polite and respectable.

And to set the tone, Cassie opened her car door, grabbed her handheld off the passenger seat and jumped out of the car before she could lose her nerve. The instant her feet hit the ground, she knew she was in trouble. Her designer pumps slipped on the ice, her body lurched back, arms flew up, head cracked the door, tailbone smacked the ice.

Yeah. Just the professional image she'd been hoping for. First, suck on a new client's tongue. Second, have him think you're a stalker. Third, fall on your ass at the start of your first scheduled session.

Excellent.

Unless she could translate all this muck into therapy? Hmm...the kiss had been to test his altruism. The stalking thing? To test his calmness under pressure. The fall?

A little tougher. Her head really hurt.

"Cassie? Are you all right?" Ty's car door slammed and she heard his feet crunch on the snow.

"Fine!" Cassie hastily grabbed the car door and hauled herself to her knees. Whoa. A little dizzy there.

What was up with him playing the gallant hero? Why hadn't he been looking down and changing the

CD or something when she fell? But no, apparently he'd been carefully watching when she'd wiped out. Typical male. Never clueless at the right time.

And to think she'd almost married one. Thank goodness she'd been spared.

Obviously, she never should have made the decision to return from the Bahamas in the first place. What was up with that inane choice? She could have bought a little hut down there and earned a living making necklaces or something. Was she an idiot or what?

SHE WAS HERE

And he was glad.

Ty scowled as he hustled around the car to check on Cassie after her header on the ice. Why was he *glad* Cassie was here? That made no sense. Sure, he hadn't been able to stop thinking about their kiss, but that kiss hadn't meant anything.

Because he was engaged.

To Alexis.

Engaged men didn't think about other women.

In actuality, he was *annoyed* Cassie was here, because he didn't need stress therapy and didn't have time for it. Especially not from Cassie. For God's sake, how could he accept therapy from someone who needed his protection from a slimy bastard? She'd been hurt and wronged and now she was trying to play the tough person? That wasn't how it worked. He'd feel like a heel asking her for help when she was the one who needed it. Not that he needed help, but if he did, he wouldn't burden her.

Cursing under his breath, he stuffed his briefcase beneath his arm as he reached Cassie—the briefcase

Alexis had given him when he'd first opened his business.

Back when they were just friends.

When life had been easier.

No, his life was just ducky now, except for the fact he was being stalked by an obsessed stress management consultant. And he wasn't happy about it. Not at all.

He scowled at her as she hung on the door. "You okay?"

She glared at him. "I said I was fine." She lifted her chin. "I didn't actually fall, you know. I was testing you."

"Yeah, right."

"It's true. I have to do some tests to ascertain the best approach for you." She sniffed haughtily. "Don't try to understand. It's really quite a complex science."

"Liar." Ty tucked his hands under Cassie's arms and hoisted her to her feet. He released her slowly... because he was worried about her maybe having a concussion and falling over, not because he liked having his hands around her waist. "You hurt?"

"Don't be ridiculous." She touched the side of her head and grimaced. "I told you I didn't actually fall."

"Want me to take you to the hospital?"

She blinked. "What?"

"The hospital. Do you need X rays or something?" Why was he feeling so damn worried about her? She wasn't his problem, and it certainly wasn't his concern if she had to go to the hospital. "I'll drive you there."

"You're worried about me?"

"Well, sure. You look like you're hurt." He'd be concerned about anyone who was hurt on his property. Cassie wasn't special. In fact, he was worried she might sue him for negligence, so all he was doing was trying to prevent a lawsuit. That was the *only* reason he was feeling all chopped up inside at the look of pain on her face.

She stared at him for a long moment. "Huh."

"Huh, what?"

She appeared to pull herself together. "Excellent work, Ty. Good response to the situation." She drew her handheld out of her pocket and flipped it open. "Very interesting." She started tapping on it with her pointer.

"Good God, not that friggin' thing again." He grabbed it out of her hand. "I really hate it when you take notes about me."

She snatched it back, her fingers brushing against his. "Too bad. That's what you hired me for."

"I fired you already."

"Didn't get that e-mail." But she didn't open the unit again. Instead, she pressed her hand to the side of her head.

He sighed. What was he supposed to do? Kick her out? "Fine. You want to come in and get some ice or something, for the head that you didn't actually hit when you didn't actually fall?"

She narrowed her eyes. "I would like to come in for our appointment."

"Give it up, Cassie. I'm inviting you in as a friend, not as a stress management consultant."

"Hey!" She glared at him. "For your information, there is no reason for you to be concerned about me on a personal level, seeing as how you're engaged to someone else and I'm not interested in men, anyway."

He blinked. "I didn't mean it like that." Or had he? No, of course not. "I just thought... You know. It's not personal or anything." Except for the fact that he couldn't stop thinking about carrying her inside and then right up the stairs to the second floor, where his bedroom was.

Good Lord! What was wrong with him? He'd worked with plenty of women on a professional level and he'd never been tempted before. Why would this be different? He wasn't a hormone-crazed adolescent. He was a boring, engaged businessman who was more than capable of having a business relationship with a woman. Even if the memory of that woman's kiss still made his body ache.

Not only was he not remotely attracted to her, but also he was completely capable of being in her presence without having any kind of sexual thoughts whatsoever, or even thinking about her as a human being. She was an aggravating stress management consultant whom he would fire before the end of the evening, and nothing more. He'd prove his immunity to her, just in case anyone was doubting him. "Come on in. I'll get you some painkillers and some ice."

She wrinkled her nose in a truly appealing fashion, then shrugged. "If I come in, it'll be for business only."

"Doesn't mean I'll listen to you." Maybe the reason he was feeling indulgent toward her was because she was vulnerable and it was natural for him to want to take care of her. Not because she was sexy or a great kisser or because he really liked her sassy attitude and total refusal to capitulate in the face of her problems.

It wasn't as if inviting her in to take care of her injuries meant he'd dump his fiancée and go after Cassie.

Holy hell! Dump his fiancée? Where had that thought come from? Alexis needed him and he would always be there for her. Wasn't that the entire point of marrying her? To be there for her forever when she had no one else? Of course.

Okay, so maybe he was a little strung out. He had to be, if he was thinking such ridiculous things. Couldn't hurt to see what Cassie had to say, just to humor her, of course. "Fine. Come in. You can talk, as long as you don't type anything into that thing."

She shrugged. "I have a photographic memory."

"Which is of course why you have to type everything into that in the first place." He held out his hand. "Give it to me."

She lifted a brow. "So, you're a control freak. Hadn't realized that."

"A control freak? Because I don't want you taking notes on me?"

"No, because you have to have my unit in your hand so you're in control of the situation." She placed it in his palm, her fingertips brushing against his skin. "Interesting."

Ty ground his teeth and said nothing. He was *not* giving her ammunition against him. So he simply turned and took Cassie's arm to escort her up the icy walkway.

"Why are you holding my arm?"

"So you don't fall. Why else would I be holding on to you?" Certainly not because he *wanted* to be touching her or anything perverse like that. He was simply being a gentleman.

"No reason," Cassie said quickly. "That's the only reason you'd touch me. I wasn't thinking anything else at all." She lifted a brow. "You like to take care of women, huh?"

"No."

"Drew never did stuff like this. I probably should've noticed, right?"

"Drew's a bastard who cheats on his fiancée."

Cheats on his fiancée. The words hung in the air as Ty guided Cassie along his front walk.

Was that what he'd done? The thought made his stomach turn to sludge, and he almost stumbled. No, he wasn't like Drew. He hadn't cheated on Alexis. The kiss with Cassie had been purely platonic, to make Drew suffer. Ty hadn't intended to enjoy it, had tried his best not to think about it since then, had even tried to convince Cassie not to help him.

But there was no doubt he'd been pleased when he'd received the message that she was coming over.

And he'd tried to work late tonight to stand her up. Then he'd found himself blowing through three red lights on the way home from the train station.

But it wasn't as if she was there on a date.

It was professional.

And the fact that he was helping her up the walk was only due to the fact that she was injured.

Nothing else.

Nevertheless, Ty released her arm promptly when they reach his front door. "I'm engaged."

She glanced at him. "I know."

He nodded. "I'm engaged."

"And I'm not deaf."

"Right." *Keep it together, Ty.* "Come on in then." He unlocked the door and pushed it open, gesturing to the front hall. "After you."

Cassie stepped inside the house and walked into the foyer. At that instant a thought struck him—Cassie was just what his house needed.

Dammit, that wasn't what he'd meant. He meant

that the house needed a woman. Not Cassie, specifically.

It would be as perfect with Alexis in it as with Cassie. No, what he meant was that it would be even more perfect with Alexis than with Cassie. No, he meant it would be perfect only with Alexis. Not Cassie.

Sleep deprivation. That was definitely the cause of his muddled thoughts. Not that he'd tell Cassie that. No doubt she'd use his insomnia as evidence that he was in need of her services.

Instead, he'd focus on something mundane that wouldn't give her more ammunition. The house. Nothing inflammatory about his house. Good, safe topic. "Sorry about the boxes. I haven't unpacked yet."

"I can see that."

Ty glanced into the living room as they walked by, suddenly seeing the house from her eyes. Boxes everywhere, furniture stashed haphazardly in random rooms. Only the couch and the television were in place—and the coffee table to put his feet on. Even the headboard to his bed was still in the front hall, propped against the closet door. Not that he cared. He certainly wasn't trying to impress her.

"How long have you lived here?"

"Six months." Now, why was he feeling as if he'd done something wrong already? So it was a house. So he hadn't unpacked. That didn't mean anything. And it didn't mean he needed to defend himself or anything. "I've been busy with work. I don't have time to get the house together."

Cassie said nothing, but he saw her glance toward her handheld, which was sticking out of his jacket pocket. "What now?" he growled.

"Nothing." She looked at him, her face a picture of innocence.

Damn, she was cute. Not that he cared. "You're judging me because my house isn't unpacked."

"Just taking mental notes."

"About what?"

"You."

He certainly wasn't remotely curious about what she had noticed about him, because that would imply weakness on his part. But maybe he'd ask just to be polite. "What exactly did you conclude?"

Cassie shrugged. "I'm assessing. Nothing to worry about."

"Assessing what?"

"You." There was the slightest hint of exasperation in her voice, but there was also a kind undertone that soothed like warm milk.

Alexis never made him think about warm milk. Ty threw his overcoat on a kitchen chair and yanked open the refrigerator door. Since when did he compare Alexis to other women? Never. It wasn't right. "Want a beer?"

"No, thanks. I'm working."

"Mind if I have one?"

"Not at all." And then she flipped open her hand-held and started clicking away.

"Where'd you get that?"

She sighed and pointed at his coat, which was hanging over a chair only a couple feet from her. "You didn't think I'd let it sit there and not get it, did you?"

Well, actually, he had. He certainly hadn't expected her to lift it out of his jacket pocket after he'd told her he didn't want her taking notes. See? That was why he was marrying Alexis. She needed him and he took care of her and that was it. Nothing complicated. Nothing like Cassie, who needed him—or *someone*—but wouldn't accept help and wouldn't do what he asked her to do.

Who needed a difficult woman like that? Not him.

She nodded at his beer. "You drink every night when you get home?"

"I'm not an alcoholic." As if it mattered to him whether she thought he was. If he wanted one beer because he was having a day from hell, then he would. It didn't mean there was anything wrong with him.

She looked up, an innocent expression on her face. "I didn't say you were."

"But you wrote down that I was going to have a beer." He selected a soda, leaving the beer on the shelf. "I'm not interested in being psychoanalyzed."

"Not many people are."

Ty glanced at the fridge, at the photograph of Alexis stuck to the front. On a whim, he pulled the photo off and handed it to Cassie, who was sitting at the kitchen table in one of the two chairs he'd actually unpacked. He pointed to the photo and said, "Alexis Hopkins. My fiancée."

Cassie took the picture, inspected it for a moment, then set it down. "Okay, Ty. I get it. You're still worried I'm stalking you. Obviously, we need to talk about New Year's Eve."

"The kiss?" *The kiss.* How could he discuss it casually, as if it was a conversation they would have in the hall next to the water cooler? No, he was fine. He didn't care about that damn kiss.

Cassie nodded. "I owe you thanks for bailing me out like that. I should never have kissed you...."

"It's okay," he said. "Really." Time to move on.

There was no need to dwell on that kiss, because doing so just made him think about how good she'd felt in his arms, how he could still taste her on his lips, how she'd kissed with a passion and commitment that had shaken him to his core and—

"Well, I appreciated it." She shifted again. "However, I understand you're engaged, and you have nothing to fear from me."

"I don't?" That was good...wasn't it? Yes, of course. Not that he was afraid of her even if she did want him. It wasn't as if he was remotely attracted to her.

"I don't have any interest in you," she said. "Except as a client." But she was looking somewhere over his right shoulder, her eyes not meeting his gaze.

As if she was lying.

His breath caught.

Had she been as affected by the kiss as he had been? *Reel it in, Ty. Don't even start thinking like that.* "That's good then," he said. "I have no interest in you, either, not even as a consultant who can cure me of all that ails me."

She looked at him then. "Still resisting my help, huh?"

"You say it like I'm in denial." Ah, much better. His stress, or lack thereof, was a safe, neutral topic.

"You are."

"I am not."

"No?" Cassie waved her arm to indicate the room. "Boxes everywhere. Paper plates and plastic utensils. You really expect Alexis to live like this?"

"I..."

"You what? Hadn't thought about it?"

"Sort of." He looked around at the boxes. It was fine for him, so why wouldn't it be fine for Alexis? She was normal and perfectly capable of living out of boxes like he was. Wasn't she?

Forget it. He wasn't going to let Cassie try to make him doubt his lifestyle. Everything was as it should be. Period.

"How many hours a week do you work?"

"A few." Now she was going after his work schedule? Did she have no sense of boundaries? Obviously not.

"Eighty?"

"Sometimes." He straightened his tie and tried not to feel as if he was disappointing her. Why in the world did it matter what Cassie thought of him? It didn't. She could think he was a workaholic slob and it wouldn't bother him in the least. Especially since there was absolutely nothing wrong with his house or his work or his fiancée or anything in his life. "What does it matter to you?"

She grinned. "You asked for my help. I already charged your credit card. So it matters a great deal to me. On a professional level only," she added quickly.

Wow. She had a really nice smile. Made him want to smile back. So he frowned. "I'm engaged."

Cassie rolled her eyes, only to flinch and press her hand to her head. "Fine. Tell me about her."

He cursed under his breath at his inability to ignore her injury anymore. He didn't like her, but he wasn't a total ogre. Keeping his face rigid and unsympathetic, he grabbed an ice pack out of the freezer and handed it to Cassie. "Here."

"You haven't unpacked any boxes, but you have ice packs?"

"I have Achilles problems."

Her face softened. "The man admits a weakness. That's a good sign."

And she jotted something else down.

That was good, right? She was happy that he'd admitted a weakness, wasn't she? So he wasn't a total beast. He wondered what she'd do if he yanked that damn unit out of her hand and read all her notes.

Not that he cared one iota what she thought of him. Nothing more than professional curiosity.

"So, tell me about Alexis," she said again.

"What about her?"

"When does she move in with you?"

"Four weeks from Sunday. February eighteenth." So soon. Too soon? No, not soon enough. "And I can't wait for my fiancée to get here. I have a fiancée." Just in case she'd forgotten.

Cassie sat up suddenly, an expression of feigned surprise on her face. "You have a fiancée? Does that mean you're engaged?"

Okay, so maybe he'd overstressed that point.

"Relax, Ty. Your virtue is safe with me." She pursed her lips, trailed her finger over the wooden table. "Trust me, I've been on the wrong side of infidelity and I'd never do that to anyone else."

Guilt settled in his gut. Here he'd been, jawing about his fiancée, when Cassie had lost hers. Ty walked over to the table, cleared his coat off the chair and sat down across from her. He might not fancy her as a person, but he owed her an apology for being an insensitive jerk. "Listen, I'm sorry for going on about my fiancée. It was rude and thoughtless."

Cassie smiled and touched his arm, sending sparks through his biceps. Not that he noticed. "No worries, Ty. This is your time, anyway. Don't worry about me."

Don't be concerned about her? The woman had nearly passed out when Drew-the-Bastard had appeared. "Let me know if he bugs you."

She lifted an eyebrow. "Why?"

"Because I'll kick his ass."

Cassie actually laughed out loud. "Are you a gallant hero or what?" She patted his arm. "I appreciate you wanting to fix my problems, but really, I'm fine. Has it occurred to you that perhaps one of the reasons you're stressed is because you're trying to save everyone around you instead of taking care of yourself?"

"What?"

"I said—"

"I heard what you said, and you're wrong. I don't try to take care of anyone. So I offered to kick his ass. So what? I would've thought you'd appreciate it. Isn't that what women want? To have someone take care of them and defend them?"

Cassie raised her eyebrow. "Some women, perhaps. I personally don't subscribe to that notion, at least anymore."

"Because Drew burned you."

She narrowed her eyes. "He didn't burn me. I'm fine. I have no issues and I don't need help."

She lifted her hand off his arm. Interesting how long she'd left it there. Even more interesting that it hadn't occurred to either of them to move. "So, tell me about Alexis."

"Alexis." He didn't want to talk about Alexis. He wanted to discuss Cassie and her issues with Drew. Which was why he was going to talk about Alexis. "I've known her since we were kids. We've been friends for over twenty years."

Cassie nodded, but didn't write anything down. "Love at first sight?"

"We've loved each other as friends since we were six." How was he going to tell Cassie that there was no romantic love between him and Alexis?

He wasn't.

It simply wasn't fair to betray Alexis like that, and it wasn't relevant, anyway. She needed him. He would take care of her. End of story.

"And when did you fall in love with her?"

Time for evasive tactics. "Two years ago her parents were killed in a car accident."

Cassie's face paled and she touched his arm again. And as before, sparks shot through him. Damn annoying. He frowned and moved his arm away. "Alexis was an only child and she was devastated."

"Of course." Cassie's voice was soft and sympathetic. Caring. The voice of a woman who would scoop up her crying child and hug him until the tears went away.

Which was great for a bawling kid. Not him. Ty certainly didn't need a compassionate woman. He took care of women; he didn't need one to take care of him. He cleared his throat. "Her parents were still supporting her while she was in school. When they died, she lost her income."

"So you started paying her tuition?"

He shrugged. "She was like my sister. I couldn't let her miss out on her dreams."

"Your sister?"

Freudian slip there. "My best friend. She's always been my best friend."

"So...you picked up her expenses. Is that when you asked her to marry you?"

"After the funeral."

"Because you didn't want her to have to go through life alone or because you loved her as a wife?"

Ty felt as though he was choking. How in the world had the conversation steered him into a dead-end alley? He'd proposed to Alexis because she'd been so sad and forlorn, standing alone at her parents' funeral without any family. He couldn't stand to see his best friend like that, so he'd told her that he would marry her, so she'd never have to be alone again.

And she'd agreed.

They'd been engaged for two years and they still had never made love.

She wanted kids, so he supposed they'd have to eventually.

Actually, he'd never seen her entirely naked. Or even partially naked.

But once she moved into his house, that would probably change.

Or maybe they'd wait until after they got married.

By then, maybe it would seem right. He'd make sure of it, because she wanted kids and he was going to give her what she wanted, dammit.

"Ty? Why'd you ask her to marry you?"

He shoved his chair back from the table and stood up. "I think you've seen enough to conclude I don't need help."

"I've seen enough to realize you don't want my help."

He scowled. "But it doesn't matter to you?"

"Not in the least." Cassie handed the ice pack to him. Unused.

Didn't she realize she wasn't so tough? Why wouldn't she accept help? It was just an ice pack. It wasn't as if she'd have to give up all her independence and freedom or anything like that. How was she going to make it on her own? He took the ice pack and threw it on the counter. It skidded across the slippery surface and off the other side, landing with a gentle *thwap* on the floor.

She lifted her eyebrow. "A little tense?"

"No."

Her other eyebrow lifted in skepticism.

He scowled.

She waited.

"Maybe I'm a little tense. But I like it. It keeps me sharp."

She smiled. "Which do you like best? Snow, cooking, board games or cleaning?"

"Who likes cleaning?"

"Some people find it soothing because when they're finished, whatever they've cleaned is...well, clean."

"Not me."

She eyed the stack of boxes next to him and a small voice inside him admitted that it would be nice to have his house unpacked. Not that he'd acknowledge it. "Snow."

"Fine. I'll be by a week from Sunday. At noon. Wear outdoor gear."

"I have to work."

"At noon on a Sunday? No wonder you're stressed."

"You work on Sundays."

She chucked him under the jaw as though he were an adorable ten-year-old. "Yes, but I like my job."

"I like mine...."

But she was already walking down the hall in her navy heels and snug-fitting navy skirt. The woman looked good in a suit, no doubt about that.

So what if being with her made him feel the most at peace he'd been in years? It wasn't because he wanted her or because her kiss still sizzled in his blood. It was simply because she was good at her job.

Wasn't it?

No need to find out. Stressed or not, he was turning her down. Some questions were better left unanswered.

"I won't be here on Sunday," he said.

"Change your mind. You won't regret it."

Not a chance.

He needed to forget about her.

Now.

5

CASSIE HUNG UP THE PHONE and glanced down at the notepad she'd been doodling on. There it was again. Ty's name written all over the page. God! What was wrong with her? It had been five days since she'd seen Ty, and she still couldn't stop thinking about him.

Tell me it's because I'm subconsciously working out a treatment plan and not because I'm obsessed with him. How could she be obsessed with him? She didn't even like men anymore, let alone want to date ever again. So she certainly wouldn't be obsessing about Ty, would she? No way. It was simply impossible.

Wasn't it? She wouldn't do anything that stupid. Would she?

Heaven help her. She couldn't even stop doubting herself now. This was all wrong. She needed to snap to it and figure out what in the world was going on.

A light tap sounded on her office door. "Cass?"

"Leo!" Leo would have answers! Cassie sat up as her friend poked her head in. "Hi!"

Leo tossed a small bag of foil-encased goodies on Cassie's desk, then plopped down in one of the client chairs. "I couldn't believe it when I drove by and saw your office lights still on. It's after nine."

"Yeah, well, my job's important. Thanks for stopping by. And for bringing chocolate." After the dismal failure of the emergency chocolate relief session, she'd decided that maybe she'd built up immunity to chocolate. She'd gone cold turkey since then. Sixteen days was enough time for all the residual chocolate to get out of her system. Time to try again. Not because she was stressed and *needed* the chocolate. Merely because she was curious as to the results of her experiment. She selected one in pale pink foil, unwrapped it and popped it in her mouth. *Heaven*. "You rock."

"So, what's up? I haven't seen you all week." Leo glanced around the office. "Did you leave the window open in a hurricane or something?"

"What?" Cassie grabbed another chocolate.

"Your office is a disaster. What happened to my anal friend?"

Cassie slowly perused the room. Hmm...stacks of files in the corner; a dirty coffee cup and the takeout container from last night still on the floor. Whoa. Why hadn't she noticed that? Failure to maintain decent standards of cleanliness was always something she looked for in her clients. Especially since she'd cleaned it last week. How had it gotten so messy already?

Leo cocked an eyebrow. "What's going on with you?"

Cassie pursed her lips. She supposed it couldn't hurt to run it by Leo and see what she thought. "Well, there's a slight possibility that I'm losing my professional edge." She lowered her voice. "I might be getting too personally involved with a client."

There.

She'd done it.

Admitted there was a chance she didn't have things in total control, as she liked to pretend.

That didn't mean she was teetering on the edge of insanity, with an inability to cope with anything. It simply indicated she was incredibly self-aware and able to assess even the smallest little blip in her oh-so-stable mental state. Not a big deal. At all.

But it never hurt to brainstorm and see what Leo would suggest.

"It's Ty, isn't it?" Leo asked.

"Lucky guess." She shoved an entire nugget into her mouth and let it melt on her tongue. *Save me, chocolate. Return me to sanity.* No, that wasn't right. That implied she'd left sanity behind when she came back from the Bahamas, which was a gross distortion of the truth. Plus she didn't need saving. Certainly not. She'd simply had a craving for chocolate just now because she was addicted and had gone too long without it. Nothing more than that.

"What's the problem?" Leo asked.

"I think I'm beginning to imagine trouble between Ty and his fiancée. He said she was like his sister and, well, that seems sort of fishy to me."

"So? That sounds like you're being an astute therapist. You're always spouting off about how marital problems are so stressful. If making love to her is like making love to his sister, then yes, that would be a problem."

Ty making love to another woman. The thought made the sweets Cassie had just eaten congeal in her stomach. A sign of being an obsessed stalker? "The thing is, sometimes when I consider that they might be having problems, I get this weird sort of feeling in my stomach, almost like I'm hoping I'm right. Probably indigestion, huh?"

"You think you might be wanting him for yourself?"

"No! That would be so unprofessional!"

"Yes, it would." Leo clucked her tongue. "Did you

consider that the sister comment could simply have meant that she's as important to him as his own sister would be? An integral part of his life and his existence?"

"Of course I considered that." How had she not thought of that? Maybe she really was obsessed with him. Maybe she was distorting reality because she couldn't cope with him actually being in love with someone else.

Great. So good to discover the negative side of being a crazed stalker: when the stalkee was in love with someone else, it sucked.

But only a little bit.

Really, it wasn't a big deal.

Because she didn't really like Ty, anyway. It was merely because he'd played the role of the hero in front of Drew. Yes, that was it. She was projecting onto him because of her own baggage. So she had a little bit of baggage. Nothing she couldn't handle.

"You going to drop him?"

Cassie frowned. "Drop Ty? Of course not."

"Why not?"

"Because he's my client. I can't abandon him in the middle of his therapy. He needs me." That was true. He did need her. As did all her clients. Nothing special about Ty.

Leo cocked an eyebrow at Cassie. "He needs you or you need him?"

"Both. I mean, he needs me. My help, that is." She rattled on before Leo could stop her and question her slip. "He's been living in his house for six months and he still hasn't unpacked. He can't remember appointments. His tie is crooked. He doesn't take care of basic home maintenance. And there's something going on

with work. Plus he threw an ice pack, and he even admitted he was tense. Oh, and he has trouble sleeping."
It's about the stress, Cassie. Nothing else. Just his stress.
That's why you've been thinking about him constantly.
"The man has some serious tension in his life."

Leo's eyes widened. "Since when do you talk about the specifics of your client's issues? You're the queen of confidentiality."

Holy shit. Leo was right. Oh, God. That was it. The first sign of total and complete mental decay. Cassie was turning in her license before she destroyed all her clients and... No. One lapse in her entire career didn't mean she'd lost all grip on her sanity, did it? She'd never make that mistake again. She'd learned her lesson. Everything was fine. If she was really bordering on psychotic, then she wouldn't have a knot of guilt in her stomach, would she? Absolutely not.

"And what about your filthy office?"

"The slightly messy office is merely an experiment to help me empathize with people who are too stressed to keep their houses sanitary. Quite brilliant, don't you think?"

"You're in denial."

Cassie frowned. "About what?"

"That you're still screwed up from that whole Drew thing. That's why you can't focus on your clients or your work or anything."

"Don't be ridiculous. I don't care about Drew." Why would she spend any time whatsoever dwelling on the man who'd had her heart wrapped around his little finger, only to tear it off, attack it with a jackhammer, throw it in the garbage disposal, then use it to clean his toilet? "You think I'm still in love with him? You've got to be kidding."

"I'm not saying you still love him," Leo said carefully. "I just think it has affected your self-confidence. It has distorted your view of relationships. You have issues."

Cassie lifted her chin. "I'm fabulous. Spectacular, even." *I am a sexy, brilliant woman whom all men yearn for. And I don't need men. Never have. Never will.* Repeated often enough, affirmations worked. Just a few thousand times more and she would believe this one.

"Are you? Maybe the reason you're obsessing about Ty is because he's safe. You're afraid of a relationship, terrified of trusting a man, so you let yourself fall for a man who's not available."

Cassie stared at Leo. "First of all, I haven't fallen for Ty. Just so we're clear on that. Second of all, where do you come up with this nonsense? I'm the stress therapist here. Don't you think I'd know if I was having some emotional collapse?"

"I'm beginning to think you wouldn't, actually."

"Well, you're wrong." Cassie sat up and spread her hands on her desk. Look at that. They weren't even shaking. Obviously, she was an emotional rock. "But your comments have helped me realize that I'm not actually obsessed with him, I don't have issues and I'm entirely capable of continuing to treat him and help him get ready for his fiancée. Ty was my rebound sexual encounter and I got a little carried away for a bit. That's it. Nothing else."

Didn't even stumble over the word *fiancée*. Did she have it together or what? She was a rock.

Leo threw up her hands. "Fine. I give. You are a testament to the fortitude of womankind."

"Exactly. I have no issues at all."

She'd just go over to Ty's house on Sunday, finish

her assessment and then prepare a treatment plan, just
as she'd do with any other client.

Because she didn't have issues.

Had she mentioned she didn't have issues?

She didn't.

CASSIE PULLED INTO Ty's driveway at 11:59 on Sunday
morning for their noon appointment. She could handle
being on time for one of their meetings because she had
no baggage with Ty.

Her hair was pulled back into a neat bun and her
flannel-lined blue jeans protected her legs from the bit-
ing wind. She wore a cute wool sweater, fleece-lined
boots with a hint of sophistication and her new
parka—warm, fitted and classy. She was the epitome
of professional and functional, and she was ready for a
de-stressing adventure.

Because that's what Ty needed, and it was her job to
provide it. All she had to do was find out what was really going on with his work and his fiancée and she'd
have all the information she needed to set up his treatment plan.

And, for those who might be wondering, she was interested in his fiancée only from a professional per-
spective. So there. And so what if she had only three
weeks to de-stress him before Alexis arrived for the fi-
nal judgment?

Twenty-one days until his fiancée would be living
with him.

Five hundred and four hours to make him fit for his
woman.

Cassie thought he was pretty good the way he was,
but she wasn't the one wearing his ring.

No, she definitely wasn't.

In fact, she wasn't wearing anyone's ring, was she? Nope. Empty hand. Bare finger. Even her tan was beginning to fade. Perhaps she'd go buy some of that tan-in-a-bottle. Hmm...not a bad idea.

Or it wouldn't be, if she cared one bit about whether any man thought she was attractive.

She didn't. To care would be to acknowledge that she needed a man to be complete, and the fact that she'd recovered so nicely from having her dreams destroyed was clear evidence that she was wonderful as an independent career woman.

Except she really missed having someone waiting for her at night.

A lump suddenly filled her throat and tears catapulted into her eyes.

What was that? *Tears?* Unacceptable. *Get it together, Cassie.* She grabbed a handful of snow and rubbed her face with it. That's right. Freeze those tears and that self-pity right out of her.

After an intolerable minute of cold, she brushed the snow away. Deep breath. All together now? Her life was *fine*. Maybe she was in a bit of a downturn. So what? It was temporary and it wasn't even a big deal and none of it even bothered her.

There. She was excellent now. Everything was groovy. Okay, back to the client. She was here for a client. It was all about the client.

Cassie squared her shoulders, marched up to Ty's house and banged on the front door with authority. She pulled the cuffs of her jacket over her hands. Idiot. How could she not have worn gloves? She still would have been a professional without frostbitten fingers.

No one answered the door.

Cassie knocked again.

Still no Ty.

Cassie shielded her eyes and peered though the window beside the door. Boxes everywhere, furniture randomly stashed. No Ty.

What was up with that? Granted, the man had said he wouldn't be here, but since when did a man say no to a woman and mean it? Impossible. If men could say no, Drew would have been as faithful and honest as... Okay, well, maybe not Drew.

"Ty!" She stepped back from the door and shouted up to the second floor. The poor man was probably curled up in a ball in the back of his closet, all wigged out from too much tension and not enough fun. "It's me! Open up!"

Again, silence. This wasn't good. He was probably comatose by now. Her breath caught. Whoa. Was he that stressed? "Ty!"

Good God. He could be having a seizure on his bedroom floor right now! "Ty!" She tried the front door. Locked.

Dammit. She had to get inside!

Cassie raced around to the back of the house and tugged on that door. Locked! How dare he have a stress attack behind locked doors. He was going to give her an attack worrying about him!

She had to get in the house and rescue him before he had a stroke. What if his fiancée arrived to find him in the hospital, paralyzed on the left side of his body? And it was all Cassie's fault! "Ty! Are you in there?"

He was probably unconscious! What if he'd had a stroke at the top of the stairs and had fallen down them and broken his neck?

That was it. She was getting inside this friggin' house *now*. Cassie ran back to the front, trying to shove open each window she passed. She was just about ready to throw herself through the glass when a window finally moved. Victory!

She pushed up the sash, flattened her palms on the windowsill and hoisted herself in. Or rather, managed to get her hips on the ledge and waggle the rest of the way in, landing on her face on the carpet inside.

Obviously, the window would have been a better option for someone who hadn't been banned from gymnastics when she was six years old because she was a danger to herself and the equipment. Totally unfair, that had been. Just because she'd gotten her elbow stuck in the trampoline and it had required a blowtorch to get her free didn't justify shutting her out. Just think, if she hadn't been expelled from gymnastics, she could have gone on to an international career and would have ended being a guest of honor in the Kremlin instead of lounging around Gardenbloom and meeting Drew.

Figured.

Cassie stumbled to her feet and looked around the room. A dining room, maybe? Tough to tell when it was filled with boxes and an assortment of tables stacked on top of each other.

No Ty.

"Ty!" Ignoring her desire to whip out her handheld and start taking notes on his housekeeping, Cassie raced through the first floor of his house. No Ty.

She shot upstairs, her breath wheezing in her chest. Good God, was she in bad shape or what? She was going to keel over from a heart attack any minute. Three bedrooms. Two bathrooms. No Ty.

Cassie stopped in the only room with a bed, her lungs burning. Okay. This was obviously his room and he wasn't there. Wasn't huddled in the closet. Wasn't on the floor having a seizure. He simply wasn't in the house.

So he was probably dead on the highway on the way home.

She whipped out her cellphone to call 911 and search the highways, but then paused. Wait a sec. It was one thing to freak out alone, but maybe it would be better to double-check her facts before calling out the National Guard.

Cassie flipped the cover on her handheld and pulled up her notes from her last discussion with Ty. Yes, she'd said she'd be here at noon today, so she hadn't gotten the time wrong. But hold on. He'd said he would be at work.

Work? No way.

With her heart starting to race, Cassie hit the speed dial on her cellphone to call Ty's office.

He answered on the first ring.

And she hung up.

Damn.

He was at work.

Not dead.

Working.

Just as he'd said he would be.

Cassie sank down onto his bed and flopped on her back, too exhausted to stand up. He was safe.

It took her almost a full minute of staring at the ceiling before the panic that had consumed her fully subsided. At which point, reality finally intruded.

"Oh my God. I have lost my mind." It was official. She'd totally and completely lost all grip on reality and sanity.

Since when did she completely fall apart with no justification just because a client missed an appointment? Never. Gross misdiagnosis of a situation. Abominable misassessment of her client's state of mind. A certain malpractice victory if she ever put such a mistake into action in her treatment.

She was a danger to herself and to others.

Was Leo right? Was it Drew? Was Cassie so screwed up that the thought of Ty standing her up for an appointment threw her into a delusional state in an effort not to acknowledge that he simply wasn't coming?

So he'd skipped an appointment. Why had she freaked out like that?

Because she was a disaster. Messy office. Obsessed with a client. Breaching confidentiality. The signs were all there. Maybe she was in the wrong profession. Maybe she wasn't stable enough to help others. Maybe her entire life had been a delusion.

No.

Cassie sat up.

Okay, she'd freaked out. It was over. No one had seen it and it was behind her now. It was a cathartic episode she'd obviously needed, but now that she'd had her release, she'd be fine.

From this moment on, she'd be in complete control of her emotions. Calm, controlled and dignified. Reserved even. People would start calling her the Cucumber because she was so cool.

The Cucumber could handle rejection.

The Cucumber wouldn't freak if a man stood her up.

The Cucumber could separate the wreck of her soul from her professional life.

No problem. She'd start wearing green, sleep in the fridge, stay away from cutting boards and she'd be all set.

Next agenda item for the Cucumber? Deal with the elusive Ty Parker. He thought he could outwit her by following through on his refusal to meet her today?

Hah. He had no idea who he was dealing with. "Ty better get ready for a battle. The Cucumber is not easily dismissed."

And the first step? Get out of Ty's house before he came home and found her lying on his bed. There'd be no talking her way out of the stalking charges then.

6

TY STRETCHED HIS ARMS over his head and yawned. Almost noon on Tuesday and he'd been at work for six hours already. Combine that with his thirteen-hour day yesterday and being at the office all weekend, and he was almost caught up.

So why was he even mentally adding up the hours? Since when did he bother to keep track?

It was Cassie. He could almost hear her voice in his head, asking him whether all those hours was a smart thing. Didn't he want to take care of his house? Didn't he worry what Alexis would think if she never saw him? *Well, forget it, Cassie. You aren't getting to me.*

He picked up a pen and tapped it on his glossy mahogany desk.

Had Cassie stopped by the house last Sunday, as she'd said she would? He couldn't believe he'd kept himself from going home and seeing if she was there. Not that he'd meet with her or anything, but he was curious. Just to see how tenacious she was. No other reason.

He didn't want her help.

He didn't need her help.

And he certainly had no interest in seeing her.

A light tap sounded on his office door.

"Come in." He tossed the pen aside and clasped his

hands behind his head, waiting for his secretary to open the door.

But it wasn't his secretary's stylish gray hairdo that peered around the door.

It was a tightly spun bun of blond hair belonging to the stress management therapist who refused to be fired. He jumped to his feet, his pulse quickening. "Cassie? What are you doing here?"

"Nice office." She stepped brazenly into the room, tapping the door shut with her toe.

She was wearing a charcoal-gray suit with practical pumps. Way too conservative for a woman of her energy and passion. She looked like a lawyer. A very attractive one with the sparkle in her eyes and the flush of her cheeks defying the stuffy image she presented. And of course, the second she opened her mouth, there was no hiding the attitude that he found so appealing. Ahem. The attitude he found so *annoying.*

"Do I make you nervous?" Cassie asked.

"Not at all. Why?"

"I think you're going to wear through the bearings on that chair if you keep spinning it around like that."

He immediately stopped swiveling. "Why are you here?"

"For our lunch date."

"What?"

"You do eat, don't you?"

"Sometimes." No way would he have forgotten lunch with Cassie. If they'd had lunch scheduled, he would have been sure to be out of the office. "But we didn't have lunch scheduled."

"We didn't? Gosh, I'm just a mess, aren't I?"

"A mess" was not the term that came to mind as he looked at the few blond tendrils escaping from her bun, her great legs and the smart-ass grin on her face. She knew damn well they didn't have lunch scheduled. He admired her audacity. And found it irritating as well. "You're not a mess," he blurted out.

"No?" She perched on the edge of his client chair, then leaned forward and propped her elbows on his desk, the cheery look on her face such a contrast to the serious, dark wood. "Do you realize I thought we had an appointment a week ago Sunday? Silly me actually showed up at your house. Can you believe that?"

She had come!

Not that he cared. "I told you I wasn't going to be there."

"I know." She flopped back in her chair like a rag doll. "And I didn't believe you. As I said, silly me. Businessmen like you don't joke about appointments, do you?"

She was so irreverent, so fun, so blissfully dismissive of the standard protocols and formalities inherent in the business world. She'd been sassy before, but today there was a new determination, a revived energy about her. He wondered what had happened to bring on that change. "You didn't love Drew, did you?"

Her face snapped into an expressionless stare. "Why do you say that?"

"Because you broke up with him six weeks ago, yet you sit here chatting away as if you have no cares in the world. You couldn't do that if you'd loved him." Why did Ty care if she'd loved Drew? It was none of his business.

Yet he didn't retract his statement. He simply waited for her confirmation.

"So, where do you want to go for lunch?" she asked instead, completely ignoring his question.

With a sudden flash of certainty he realized he'd never tire of her spunk and her total disregard for his attempts to control her. She had a fire and a zest for life he'd forgotten existed.

"I have a lunch meeting," he said. Didn't he? "And I have to work, anyway." He jerked his head at the stack of files on his desk.

"Where's your boss? I'll talk to him."

He chuckled. "I have no doubt you would. But I don't have one."

"You don't?" She eyed him. "You own this company?"

"Actually, yes. I work for myself. I share office space with the other folks here. My secretary is the only one in my employ."

"Really? Huh." Cassie pulled out her handheld and jotted down a few notes.

"Huh, what?" For the first time, instead of being annoyed with her note taking, a warm lump settled in his stomach.

She cared.

So what if it was because he was paying her?

The simple fact was that she cared whether he was okay.

And he liked it.

"I'm engaged."

"Oh for heaven's sake, not that again." She walked over to the door and pulled his wool overcoat off the hook. "Put this on and let's go. I'm hungry, and when I get hungry I get ornery. It's not a pretty sight."

"You, ornery? Hard to imagine."

"Sarcasm, huh?" She nodded sagely. "Always an attractive trait."

"Back at ya."

She grinned. "Just seeing if you were listening to me or mooning over Alexis's face in your mind."

"I don't moon."

"You should."

"Why?"

"If I was about to get married, I'd want my fiancé to moon about me."

"Would you moon about him?"

"Of course I would."

"Did you moon about Drew?"

She stiffened. "Irrelevant."

"How is it irrelevant? We were discussing mooning over fiancés. Drew was your fiancé, so it was completely logical to ask whether you'd mooned over him."

Cassie lifted her delicate chin. "It's irrelevant because the focus of our interaction is you and your issues. Not me and my issues. Not that I have issues," she added quickly. "Because I don't."

"I don't, either."

Cassie narrowed her eyes at him and he felt as if she were stripping away his skin to peer into his soul. "I'm not an idiot, Ty. I know you're not fine."

"Is anyone totally fine? Are you? A little stressed about your recent breakup, I imagine?"

Cassie scowled. "Why does everyone think I'm upset about Drew? The guy's a jerk. I'm over him."

"So, you have some stress in your life, but you're totally capable of dealing with it. Is that what you're saying?"

She blinked. "I may have been upset for a day, but that's it. I'm fine."

"Exactly. As am I. Entirely capable of dealing with the issues in my life."

Cassie narrowed her eyes. "Okay, Ty, I'll make a deal with you. Come to lunch with me. Answer a few questions. If you convince me that you have a handle on everything and you really don't want my help, I'll walk away." She grinned. "But I'm keeping the money."

She held out his overcoat and waited.

Easy enough. Answer a few questions, then be done with Cassie forever. Hell, why did that thought make him angry? He would be glad to have Cassie out of his life, and he'd prove it by going to lunch with her and answering her questions.

And next time, he wasn't paying up front. That took all the control away from him. If he hadn't paid, he could withhold payment and she'd have no choice but to leave him alone or risk working for free.

He grabbed the coat out of her hand, his fingers brushing against hers.

"And for your information, I always make my clients pay up front, because it's not uncommon for them to want to fire me partway through, so don't think you're anything special." She flipped him a grin over her shoulder as she walked out his door.

Great. That's all he needed, for her to turn clairvoyant on him. As if she wasn't getting under his skin enough already.

As he walked out the door, he caught the faintest scent of something flowery and feminine. Deliciously tantalizing.

This was going to be a long lunch.

CASSIE TRIED TO FOCUS on her treatment plan as Ty guided her along the sidewalk with his hand on her elbow. He'd even made sure to walk closest to the street in case a wayward cab came over the curb to take them out. Of course, it wasn't because she was special or anything. It was simply his way. But it certainly was making it difficult for her to concentrate on what she wanted to accomplish over lunch.

Let's see... Right. Info about work and Alexis. Simple enough. Two questions and then she could be outta there before lunch even arrived.

Not that she was planning to bolt or anything. The extra week she'd taken to regroup before coming after Ty was plenty of time to leave the psychotic episode behind. She hadn't freaked out once since then. Because she'd moved past that. For example, she wasn't thinking about how good it felt to have Ty's hand on her elbow, how protected she felt with him beside her....

Ack! Hadn't she just said she *wasn't* thinking about that?

Ty reached for the tinted glass door to the restaurant and held it open for her. "This place okay?"

"Sure." She stepped inside, her shoulder grazing against his chest. Not on purpose! She wasn't some psycho trying to cop a feel whenever she got a chance!

Think about something other than Ty. Okay, she could do this, even though he had his arm around her shoulders to protect her from the crowd of executives packed in the foyer waiting for tables. Cellphones rang, voices rose over the din while bodies jostled for a good spot against the wall. It was just like going to lunch with Drew.

Whoa. Drew. Was that really a better topic to occupy her mind than thinking about how she'd just been bumped so she slammed into Ty's chest and got a good whiff of his aftershave?

Get it together, Cassie. This was a business lunch. Remember the Cucumber? No thinking about the wreck of her life when with a client. No inhaling Ty and no thinking about the beast she'd almost married. She'd just start a neutral conversation to pass the time until they could sit down and start dissecting Ty. "Same ol' thing, huh?"

"As what?" Ty nodded at the maître d', who gave him a quick smile before he turned to check his little black folder.

"I used to meet Drew for lunch in the city every Wednesday. It was like this place." Now, what was that about? Hadn't she just decided she wasn't going to think about that jerk? Point of clarification: when she banned herself from thinking about him, it also included talking about him.

Noted for future reference. Her mouth wouldn't make that mistake again. There would be no more thinking or talking about Drew.

"So, you used to drive all the way into the city to have lunch with Drew?" Ty folded his arms and studied Cassie, using his bulk to block her from the crowds.

Now, why had he gone and asked about Drew? She'd made it an entire millisecond without thinking about him and then Ty had gone and brought him up again. Men. So insensitive.

"Cassie?"

No, this was good. She could use it as practice: learn to speak about Drew without getting violent. "Yes, I used to meet him in the city for lunch." Not even a quiver in her voice. She was so tough. Like iron.

"Why?"

Cassie frowned. "Because it was the only time we could see each other. He got a promotion and had to stay in the city during the week, so I came in for lunch to see him." Look at her! The words flowing easily. The incident at Ty's house had clearly been an aberration, probably caused by eating some bad food or something.

Ty raised an eyebrow. "He was sleeping in the city all week? He couldn't make the hour trip from Gardenbloom?"

"Yes. He had to work...." Her voice faded at the skeptical look on Ty's face. "What?"

"Nothing." He nodded at the maître d'. "Our table is ready." Ty placed his hand on Cassie's back to guide her through the crowd. "After you."

"Why'd you give me that look?"

"No reason. This way."

Ty was holding out on her. What was weird about Drew staying in the city? Drew making time for her each week had been a sign of his true love...except there hadn't been true love. He'd been a lying, deceitful skunk....

Whoa. Cassie stopped and Ty plowed into her. "Cassie? What are you doing?"

Had Drew's little lunch date each week been a ploy to assuage any suspicions about his new late hours? Had his extracurricular wandering happened more than just the night before their wedding? Had it been going on for the last two years?

"Cassie? Are you okay?" Ty folded his hand around her upper arm, his grip firm and supportive. "You look a little pale."

"I...just had a...revelation...."

"A bad one, from the look on your face." He tightened his hold on her. "Let's go sit down."

"No..." She tried to pull out of his grasp. "Not here."

"Nonsense, the food is great. I eat here all the time."

"Ty..." Her legs were wobbling and the room was spinning. Had she been a total fool?

Apparently.

Drew had been cheating on her for two years. At least. Of that she was suddenly certain. Late nights? Spending four nights a week in town because he was working so late? An incredibly doting lunch each week to pamper her and make her feel adored?

She was such an utter imbecile.

A trusting, naive idiot.

She was the kind of woman she'd always pitied.

How many other people had known?

Had the people at his office Christmas party snickered behind her back?

"This way, Cassie."

She stumbled past the tables, kept vertical only by Ty's increasingly strong grip. It was as if he sensed her weakness, knew she needed his support. She wanted to scream at him to take her out of there, but she couldn't.

How could she ask for help? Admit weakness? She was his consultant, for heaven's sake. She had to project the ultimate confidence and satisfaction with life. Being needy wasn't allowed.

"Sit here." Ty maneuvered her into a chair, then pushed it in for her.

He sat across from her, then leaned close. "What in the world is wrong with you?"

"Nothing." *Be strong. Be powerful. Drew's not worth it.*

"Don't even try to lie to me." Ty's brows were furrowed in concern; a muscle ticked in his cheek. "Talk."

Cassie took a deep breath.

She picked up a crystal goblet and gulped her water.

Then she set down her glass.

On the edge of her plate.

Only Ty's quick grab kept the glass from tipping over and gushing its contents all over the white linen tablecloth.

"Cassie! What's going on?"

The room was so crowded.

Silverware clinking.

Dress shoes clicking on the hard floor.

There were so many people.

Talking.

Laughing.

Loud.

So loud.

She pressed her fingers to her temples and closed her eyes.

And she began to count to a hundred.

She felt Ty's presence as he leaned across the table, his head huddled next to hers, his breath warm against her cheek. He lowered his voice. "Cassie. What are you doing?"

"Counting to one hundred."

"Why?"

"So my head doesn't explode and fall off."

"I don't think there's much of a chance that's actually going to happen."

"I beg to differ."

Ty's hands closed over hers and he pulled her fingers away from her temples. "Cass. Look at me."

Cass. He'd called her Cass. An endearment, as if they had a special connection. And unfortunately, it made her feel all too warm and snuggly inside. At the same time, it made her want to run screaming from the room because they *didn't* have a special connection. No one was her special someone. She was *alone.*

Which was good, right? She didn't want anyone. And she hadn't married Drew, had she? No. So that was good, too.

She took a deep breath, plastered a smile on her face and looked up. Her breath caught in her throat as she realized Ty's face was still only inches away. He was so close she could almost feel his lips on hers.

For a long moment they froze, the sounds of a crowded restaurant fading until it was only them.

Then Ty cleared his throat and leaned back in his seat. "So, what's wrong?"

How she wanted to drop her independent facade and tell him all about the muck crowding her heart.

But she couldn't.

She was being paid to help him, not to dump her problems on him. At the very least, she would maintain composure until she had the privacy to fall apart, if that's what she needed to do. Not that she *would* crumble. After all... "I am the Cucumber."

Ty nodded. "I suspected as much."

Cassie frowned. "What?"

"Just trying to follow your lead. Not really sure where the cucumber thing is going, though."

She almost smiled. Funny guy. "Tell me about your job."

His eyes darkened. "You won't tell me what's wrong?"

"Nothing's wrong."

"Don't lie to me."

He sounded offended that she'd lie to him. What did it matter if she hid things from him? She had no obligation to confess her secrets to him. Yet at the same time, she could still feel his supportive grip on his arm as he'd led her through the crowded restaurant. He cared about her.

As a friend, only, of course.

But he did care.

He was probably solicitous of everyone.

He was that kind of man.

And he deserved to have that recognized. So, how to do it without actually revealing that she was anything other than an emotional rock? A brick? A cement block? "Fine, Ty. I may have a very small issue, but I'm not interested in discussing it right now. We're here to help you."

He nodded and his shoulders relaxed, and she knew then it would always be better to tell him the truth. He was that kind of guy. She supposed it was a good thing to be forced to acknowledge that there was at least one man on the planet who valued honesty.

"If you want to talk about it, I'm here," he said.

And he would be.

She was certain of it. Honest and dependable. Huh. Hadn't really thought those traits were actually part of the male genetic make up. Or maybe Ty wasn't really male. Maybe he was an alien from another planet. Yes, that was it. A much more logical explanation. She smiled. "Thanks."

"I mean it."

"I know." She hesitated. "Alexis is a lucky woman."

"No, she's not."

How about that? His denial wasn't driven by modesty or humility. He definitely believed his words. Interesting. "Why isn't she lucky?"

"Because her parents died two years ago."

"But she has you."

"It's not the same."

"No, it's not. But you're her present and her future. Your love will make her life wonderful."

Ty's face darkened and he tightened his grip on his water glass.

"Ty?"

"I don't want to talk about love."

Ah. A problem area? "Why not?"

"You asked me about my work."

"Yes, I did." She'd also asked him about love, but she opted not to point that out right now. Timing. It was all about timing. "Tell me about work."

"I opened my own business ten years ago."

"And how is business?" Look at her go! Interrogating her client with top-notch finesse. She was back and she was better than ever. Was she resilient or what?

"Business is great."

"Do you love your job?"

A definite flinch before he answered. "Yes."

Aha! *We uncover the crux of the problem.* "If you didn't have to earn money and could have any job you wanted even if it paid nothing, what would you do?"

"Open a pizza place," he said without hesitation.

Whoa. Hadn't seen that one coming. "A pizza place?"

He nodded. "The kind you find in small towns. Quaint, homey. Where everyone in town goes for the best pizza in six counties, but only the owner knows what's in the sauce and the crust. It's a secret that keeps everyone coming back."

"Is that why you bought a house in Gardenbloom? Because someday you want to do that?" Ty was a down-home pizza boy. She'd never have thought it. Did that mean he'd build tree houses for his kids, too?

Whoops. Interjecting personal fantasies into business. Never a good thing.

"I bought the house for Alexis."

Alexis. Why did that name make Cassie want to leap up and engage in violent behavior? Interesting. "She wants to live in Gardenbloom?"

"She should be in a suburb."

"Why?"

"Because that's what she deserves."

"And it has nothing to do with what you want?"

Ty's face darkened. "My job is to take care of her. Period."

Okay, then. Cassie guessed she knew how he felt about that. "So, what about the pizza place? Have you told her about that?"

He looked past her. "Not really."

"Given it the ol' drive-by to see if she slows down and gives it a ride?"

"Sort of."

"And let me guess. She hit the gas?" How could a woman possibly be opposed to her husband ending his commuting life to set up a charming pizza place five minutes from home? It was perfect! They could set up a little nursery in the back, so Mom and Dad and baby could all bond together and...

"She needs security."

She who? What was Ty talking about? Oh, right. That woman he was engaged to, the one with the bad name.

"Which is totally understandable," he continued. "Since her parents died, her life has been...uncertain."

"So, let me see if I have this. You want to quit your job to open a pizza place, and Gardenbloom would be perfect. But your fiancée wants you to keep working at a job you don't love so you'll bring in the big bucks and put her up in style?'' Sounded like a keeper to Cassie. Perhaps she should get Alexis together with Drew. And then who would be with poor Ty? As his consultant, Cassie supposed she could extend her services to grief counseling to help him cope with being single....

Ty shifted. ''She didn't exactly say that. It's just a feeling I got from her.''

''Well, no wonder you're stressed.'' Seriously. Cassie was really liking the plan of getting Drew and Alexis together. D. & A. Those initials could stand for Dumb-Ass. Interesting coincidence. ''I think you need to have a talk with Alexis and tell her what you want.''

''And put that kind of burden on her? No way.''

Was he a hero or what? Willing to shoulder a heavy burden for the woman he loved. Maybe Ty should conduct training classes for teenage boys, to teach them how to be decent human beings before they reached the age where they teased women with promises of happily ever after. ''How do you know it'll be a burden? You just said you were guessing as to her response.''

''We've been friends for over twenty years. I *know* her.''

''Do you really?'' Now he was the one being naive. Obviously, it was up to Cassie to help guide him toward reality. Ah, reality. What a cruel and ugly place it could be without a fabulous stress management consultant to ease the reentry. Good thing she could self-treat or she might have found herself in a bit of a pickle. ''Perhaps you're so stressed because you're trying to save her from the world, yet you don't even know if she needs saving. Might be worth it to actually ask her what she wants." Men. Such an aversion to communication.

Ty glared at her. "The entire reason for marrying her is to eradicate her problems, not add to them."

"I thought the reason for marrying someone was love," Cassie said.

Interestingly enough, the man looked rather like a volcano the instant before an eruption, with his flushed cheeks, black eyes and ticking cheek muscle. But he didn't explode. He simply said, "I said I wasn't interested in talking about love."

"Right. That keeps slipping my mind. My apologies." Very interesting. Perhaps that "sister" comment he'd made earlier had some significance. Or maybe Cassie was so desperate for a man that she was projecting her psychotic delusions on him.

"I don't believe you," he said.

"That I'm sorry or that it keeps slipping my mind?"

"Both."

She smiled. "Well, you're right. It's my job to dig until I find out what's bugging you. And I think I'm getting an idea."

"It's not Alexis."

As if Cassie could be that lucky, to have his relationship with Alexis be a problem.

Whoa.

What was that?

A little personal longing interfering with her business?

Not appropriate.

Not permissible.

Not going to happen again.

Especially since she wasn't about to trust any man with any part of her body, mind or soul *anyway.* Since she was going to stay solo, what was the point of fabricating trouble between Ty and his fiancée? No point at all. Who wanted a man, in any case? Not her.

Cassie tilted her head and studied Ty, noting his enviously thick eyelashes. Was Leo right? Was that why she was so attracted to him? Because he was taken and, therefore, safe to fantasize about, since she'd never have to risk giving her heart to him? That led to embarrassing revelations about her hostility toward the name Alexis.

None of it mattered, anyway, because Cassie wasn't going to entertain any more fantasies about him.

Nope. Done. Over. Finis. Kaput.

She was moving on.

Or moving nowhere.

Nowhere was safer.

And safe was what she wanted right now.

7

TY RUBBED HIS EYES as he turned the corner to his house. It had been a long week, but he'd finally made it to Friday. He'd worked until midnight almost every night, barely stumbling into his bed before he was up again.

And he'd hardly thought about Cassie and their lunch together.

And he hadn't been wondering why he was still working so hard after all these years, still saving money. For what? The pizza place he'd never open? So, if he wasn't going to start making pizza, why was he trying to earn so much money?

For Alexis.

Part of his obligation as a husband was to provide a safe and secure home. Marrying Alexis was about taking care of her. And it didn't matter that it wasn't about love, despite what Cassie would say about marrying someone you didn't love. He had no doubt that Cassie was someone who would love her husband deeply and completely forever, and she would think it was horrible for him to marry Alexis for any reason other than love.

Well, it wasn't.

Love like the kind Cassie would give her husband wasn't what Ty wanted.

Nope.

Nope.

Nope.

Cassie! His headlights illuminated her Subaru, which was parked across his driveway.

He hadn't seen her or heard from her in the three days since their lunch together.

Not that he'd been counting.

His heart racing, he slammed his car into Park and jumped out. He hustled carefully across the icy driveway and peered in her window. Her head was back against the seat, her eyes closed, her mouth parted in sleep. The engine was idling softly, probably keeping the car warm while she waited for him.

She'd waited for him.

It made his blood thicken with warmth.

He smiled, thinking how wonderful it would be to wake up to that face, to be able to bring her breakfast in bed on Sundays, how she'd throw her arms around him in genuine and loving appreciation.

Good God! What he thinking? Was he insane?

"Cassie! Wake up!" He scowled and banged his fist on the window.

She jerked upright and glanced his way. When she saw him, she smiled and rolled down the window. "Hi, Ty. Got plans tonight?"

"What's wrong?" Her eyes looked tense and her voice sounded strained.

"What?" She blinked. "Nothing." She flicked her automatic locks and unlocked the doors. "Hop in. We're going on a field trip."

She was lying. Something was bothering her. "Cassie…"

"It's almost nine. We need to get going."

"Fine." If she didn't want to discuss it, then he

didn't, either. It wasn't like he cared about her or anything. "Where are we going?"

"Surprise."

"What kind of surprise?"

"Relax, Mr. I'm Engaged. It's business."

"Part of my stress management therapy?"

"What else?"

He had to admit he wasn't feeling particularly
stressed anymore. Didn't even care about taking his
laptop inside and settling down to finish some work.
To be honest, he rather felt like having an adventure.
After all, it was Friday night. No harm in taking off a
Friday night every six years or so.

Especially if it meant he could spend some time with
Cassie.

Not because he was interested in her.

Simply because she made him feel good.

Because she was good at her job.

No other reason.

"Fine. I'll come."

SHE WAS SO EXCITED about tonight. Her brilliance as a
stress therapist was about to be unveiled. Sure, it was a
big step, but Ty was ready. It was going to be great
and...

"Um, Cassie?"

She noticed Ty's hand wrapped around the door
handle. "You want to know where we're going, don't
you?" As usual, she could read her client's mind. That
was part of what made her so fabulous at her job.

"Actually, no. I was wondering if you were familiar
with the phrase 'driving to endanger'?"

So her clairvoyant capabilities weren't impeccable.
They were still highly tuned weapons that made her

the envy of all her competitors. "I'm not driving fast." She flinched as she noticed the big Do Not Enter sign on the road she was turning onto. Nice timing. "This street isn't really one-way. It's just a red herring the residents installed to decrease traffic."

Ty double-checked his seat belt. "So...did you know you could be convicted of voluntary manslaughter if I died as a result of your reckless driving?"

"I'm not going to kill you. Are you a wimp? Too stressed out for a little fun?" She never would have pegged Ty for a wimp. Huh. She wasn't even driving over the speed limit. Come on, she had a client in the car. Would she really endanger someone in her care? Never. "You need to relax, Ty."

"Did you see that speed limit sign we just passed?"

Cassie tried to think. "Maybe."

"Did you notice it said thirty miles per hour?"

"It's likely. This is a residential area."

"Look at your speedometer."

Cassie sighed with exasperation. "Lighten up. I thought men were supposed to like speed...." She caught sight of the speedometer. Sixty-three? Yikes. She immediately eased her foot off the pedal. "I'm sure it's broken."

"Your sense of self-preservation or the speedometer?"

She wrinkled her nose as she watched the passing snowdrifts come into focus as the car slowed down. "Hmm. Maybe I was going a little fast."

Ty took a deep breath and unwrapped his fingers from the door handle. "Ordinarily, I'm not averse to speeding. But you're driving thirty miles over the speed limit. In a neighborhood. The wrong way down a one-way, curvy street. And there's snow on the road.

Might be pushing the boundaries of sanity just a little bit, don't you think?''

Note to self: the mental collapse at Ty's house when she'd thought he was comatose upstairs had not entirely healed itself. Unfortunately, this time there was a witness. How could she purport to be Ty's salvation when she was so deranged she couldn't manage to sustain even a tenuous grip on the normal boundaries of societal behavior? Unless... "I did it on purpose. It's part of your therapy." Apparently, her subconscious had created the therapy plan. Irrefutable evidence of her natural talents for this business.

"Flirting with death is part of my therapy?"

"Yep." She paused for a full five-second count at a stop sign. See? She was in complete control.

Ty folded his arms and eyed her as she very gently pressed the gas to nudge the car into a leisurely crawl down the road. "Tell me how making me fear for my life, as well as yours, could possibly reduce my stress level in any way? I'm really not making that connection."

"You weren't thinking about work, were you? A top-notch distraction." That really was excellent therapy. She'd have to engage it in the future with other clients. Nothing like fearing for your life to make the rest of your problems seem insignificant. "Feel free to call me a genius."

Ty raised an eyebrow. "How many clients have you killed?"

"None."

"How many have you sent to the hospital?"

"Two, but one of them really wasn't my fault. And it was when I was first starting out and experimenting with therapies. That's the foundation of my success. In-novation."

"Cassie."

She shot a glance at him. "What?"

"What's up with you tonight?"

"I'm trying to save you. Just doing my job. Nothing going on with me." Yeesh. Why *did* people make such a big deal over little things?

"Okay..." He shifted in his seat so he could face her. "You want to be evasive? I can dig."

"I'm not interested in talking about myself, thanks so much for the offer."

"How long were you waiting for me?"

"Not long." So much for the man taking a hint. As if she would have expected him to be agreeable. He was a man, for heaven's sake. Granted, he actually seemed to be trustworthy and loyal, but still. That didn't make him a saint.

"Cassie."

Why *did* he have to be so intolerant of lies and so good at spotting them? It was very annoying. "Fine. I was waiting for a couple hours."

"A couple hours. Why?"

"I didn't know what time you'd be home."

"You could have left me a message."

"True. Forgot you had a phone."

"Don't believe you. Try again."

Cassie paused at a red light and rubbed her chin. "Forgot I had a phone."

He chuckled. "Strike two."

Her mind was a complete blank, utterly devoid of any even semiplausible excuses. So...might as well opt for the truth. She was too tired for anything else. It had absolutely nothing to do with the fact that she simply couldn't cope anymore and would take the opportunity to talk to a drunken gigolo if he'd listen to her. "I had a bad day and didn't want to be at home anymore."

"What happened?" There was genuine concern in his voice, not voyeuristic curiosity, which made her desperately want to confide in him.

She sighed and turned right on Main Street. Maybe listening to her problems would be therapeutic for him.... Surely she could turn this into something professional, not a needy plea for help from the person she was supposed to be saving. Let's see...if she told him about her problems and he tried to help her, then they would bond and he'd feel more inclined to confide in her. And only with his trust would she truly be able to help him.

Excellent plan. It was all for the client's sake. "Drew called."

Ty grunted. "Tonight?"

"Yes. He...wants to get back together." What did Ty's grunt mean? Disgust that she'd taken Drew's call? Raging jealousy because he wanted her for himself?

"And what did you say?" His voice was quiet, but it made the hair on her neck stand up.

Cassie pulled up in front of an empty storefront and shifted into park. "I hung up on him."

"Good." Ty peered at her. "Not good?"

She bit her lip. *Be strong, Cassie. Don't burden him.* Sure, she'd figured out how to make her confessions be for his own growth and development, but come on! It really wasn't that easy to be the one talking. Much better to scream into her pillow and scarf down a pan of brownies. "We're here."

"Tell me what's bugging you."

Cassie sighed and let her head flop against the seat. Okay, fine. It was just way too much effort to resist his demands. Obviously, in order to heal, he needed to hear about her problems. For him, she'd do it. Her altruism was astonishing. "I finally realized that he'd been cheating on me for several years, not just that one time thing before my wedding."

"So...why feel bad? You ditched the guy before you married him."

"Because I feel like an idiot! I trusted him!"

"Ohh..."

Floodgates were open now. No stopping. All for Ty's sake, of course. "When he spent four nights a week in the city for work, I believed him. When he told me he had to take business trips, I trusted him. When women would call the house about a work crisis, I didn't question it. And I feel like such a fool."

"Whoa." Ty brushed her hair out of her face, a tender and soothing touch that made her want to handcuff him to her and keep him with her until she healed. Ahem. Until *he* healed. This was all about him. "Cassie, the guy's an ass. Just be glad you got out before you were stuck with him."

"But I trusted him, and I was an idiot! How am I supposed to know whether the next guy I like is a decent human being?"

Ty released her and leaned back against the seat. "Ah."

"Ah? What does that mean?" Whoops. She was getting a little hostile—and it had absolutely nothing to do with being grouchy because he was no longer giving her comforting love-touches. Time for the emergency stash. "Can you open the glove box for me?"

"Not all guys are untrustworthy," Ty said as he opened the compartment.

"Hand me the item wrapped in gold." Thank heavens she'd reloaded yesterday. The last couple of months had taken quite a toll on her chocolate relief fund.

He did as directed. "Most men probably are worth trusting, actually."

"And how am I supposed to tell the good ones from the bad ones?" She unwrapped the foil, revealing a two-inch piece of mint fudge. Hopefully she was over her chocolate immunity. "I was with Drew for four years and I never noticed a blond hair that wasn't mine or a scent of perfume I'd never wear."

"He was a skilled practitioner of the art of being a lying, cheating scumbag," Ty said, but there was no admiration in his voice. Good thing or she would have pushed him out of the car and left him on the sidewalk to freeze to death.

She broke off a piece and let it melt in her mouth. Chocolaty mint seeped into her body, caressed her tongue. *Drew, Drew, go away. Never come back any other day.* "So, how do I tell if the next guy is a liar?" Assuming, of course, she ever went back to the fountain of love for another swim. Which was an awfully big assumption. In fact, it was really more of a hypothetical question.

"I'll screen him," Ty said.

"You?"

"Sure. Men can read other men no problem. I'd know in a minute if he was honest."

Cassie eyed Ty while she ate another piece of fudge. "How would you know?"

Ty rubbed his chin and gazed out at the street, which

was occupied by only a few hardy souls, braving the cold weather and rushing into the two restaurants on that block. "I'm not sure. Maybe because men tend to...brag about stuff like that? Not necessarily aloud, but they project that message to other guys."

"Men are despicable."

"Some. Not all."

"Would you ever cheat on Alexis?"

"Never."

"What if you found your true love and you were already married to Alexis?"

He looked at Cassie sharply. "What makes you think I'm not marrying my true love?"

"I'm just speaking hypothetically." Or she had been...but his quick retort was intriguing.

"Speaking hypothetically, no. No matter what, I'll be faithful to her."

"Alexis is a lucky woman." Oops. Cassie sounded just a little too wistful there...as if she wished she were the one Ty had dedicated himself to. "I mean, because she has someone she can trust."

"There are others who are trustworthy."

"Who?"

Ty raised an eyebrow. "You mean, do I know other men who wouldn't cheat on their wives?"

"Yes. Do you?" She was beginning to believe that Ty was indeed trustworthy, but she was also quite certain that he was one of a kind. Should be in a museum, actually. Studied by scientists as a freak of nature.

"Of course." Then he cocked his head. "Want to meet one?"

"A date?" She grew cold and her hands became clammy. "I'm not ready for a date."

"Maybe you are. Maybe you need to get out there and realize not all men are like Drew."

"Why does it matter to you whether I date?"

"Because then you wouldn't be available."

"Available for what?"

Ty's face suddenly darkened into a scowl. "I just mean, you're a nice person and you deserve someone. And if you're involved with someone, then...I won't have to..."

"Won't have to what?" Her lungs were tight with anticipation. He wouldn't have to dream about her at night? *Say it, Ty!*

No! Don't say it, Ty! If he had feelings for her, then he'd be betraying Alexis, and Cassie needed to know there was some man out there who could be trusted, even if he wasn't with her. At the same time, she hadn't been able to stop her own dreams about him, and if he felt the same way about her... No! Then he would be unfaithful to Alexis.

Arrgh!

"Then I won't have to worry about you," he said. "As a friend."

Relief and regret washed over her. "Ah, yes. As a friend." No way was she feeling bad just because Ty wanted to set her up with another man. That would be ridiculous. He was engaged to another woman and she didn't want him to betray her. Not to mention she wasn't going to start dating for at least a century, anyway.

"Have faith, Cassie."

"I had faith and that's how I ended up nearly marrying the jerk."

"He's more than a jerk."

"How about...scheming dirtbag?"

"You can do better than that."

Cassie rubbed the back of her hand on her chin. "A stupid stupid excuse for a man?"

"I thought you were creatively inspired?"

"Lily-livered leech sediment?"

He grinned. "Getting there."

"Yellow-bellied turtle heiny?" Hmm. This was rather liberating. Inspiring actually. "Fetid cottage cheese head?"

"Feels good, huh?"

"It does, actually. I can insult him, but maintain a sense of humor so I don't plunge into a pit of pointless despair and self-pity." Cassie grinned. "This is the first time I've actually felt like laughing when referring to the noxious miasma of putrefying roadkill I almost married."

"Best one yet. For that, I might even concede to your self-proclaimed genius status."

She laughed and stretched her arms over her head, realizing that the tension was gone from her shoulders and her headache had subsided for the first time since Drew had called three hours ago. The result of the chocolate or the bonding with Ty?

She had a feeling it hadn't been the chocolate. The teacher had become the student and been bested. For the moment. She still reigned supreme when it came to de-stressing. And she would prove it. "Okay, are you ready for your surprise, or what?"

EVEN IF THE SURPRISE was pushing him off a bridge into a raging, freezing river that would paralyze his lungs instantly as it swept him to his death, Ty decided it would be safer than any further discussion on Cassie's need to start dating again.

Thinking about her dating another man made him miserable. Which was why he needed to set her up with someone. To get her on another man's arm so Ty wouldn't sit there thinking about how she was alone and how deserving she was of someone to love her....

"In here." Cassie walked to the front of a darkened shop and inserted her key in the door. Brown paper was taped over the inside of the windows and the interior was dark.

The word *Smiley's* was written on the window in big gold letters, but the place looked more like an abandoned den of depression than an operation that would make anyone smile. "Why are we here?"

Cassie just grinned, her face barely lit by the streetlights. "You'll see." Her key turned in the lock and she pushed the door open. "Come in."

She reached to her left and flicked on the lights. It was an old, classic ice-cream parlor. Abandoned, dusty, it came complete with the fountains and bright red stools at the counter and a black-and-white-checkered floor.

"Why are we here?" he asked again.

Cassie pushed the door shut with her toe, grabbed Ty's arm and pulled him into the middle of the room. "Don't you see? Doesn't it have charm?"

"If you ignore the half-inch layer of dust on everything...I suppose."

"Ty! Imagine this place with pizza instead of ice cream."

He reeled backward as if she'd struck him. "What?"

"This place. It could be your store! There's a big kitchen out back where they used to make ice cream. You'd have to remodel, but there's a lot of work space back there." She sashayed across the floor, her arms held out as if she were ice skating to a lyrical tune. "Imagine folks sitting at the counter, eating their pizza, chatting with you while you made their drinks. Others lounging at tables, warm and cozy. Homey." She stopped at the row of stools and whirled around, her cheeks flushed and her eyes glowing. "What do you think?"

He loved it. It was perfect. He could practically smell the pizza dough rising on the counters, browning in the ovens. The heavenly scent of fresh garlic and oregano. The murmur of familiar voices, of regulars who told him about their day, whose kids he knew.... It was everything he'd dreamed.

And he had to let it go.

For Alexis.

Before he'd seen this place, it had been such a distant dream. But now, it was a reality. With a snap of his fingers, he could have this space and begin making his dream take shape.

"Dammit, Cassie. Why did you do this?"

"What?" The sparkle faded from her eyes and he instantly felt guilty.

But he couldn't help it, couldn't take back the sharpness.

So he turned and walked out, leaving the most thoughtful woman he'd ever met standing in the dust by herself, with only his guilt to keep her company.

8

HE WAS ALREADY TWO BLOCKS from the shop by the time Cassie caught up to him in her car. The collar of his wool overcoat was pulled up over his ears, his hands shoved deep in his pockets. To say he looked annoyed would be a slight understatement.

Cassie slowed her car and rolled down the passenger window. "Why are you mad?" Of course she knew why, but this was part of the therapy. Force him to acknowledge his feelings. Someday he'd appreciate what she was doing for him.

Unless her professional sensibilities were still off-kilter and she'd actually made a horrible mistake bringing him here...

"You want to know *why*?" Ty stopped and whirled toward the car. "What kind of a stress management therapist are you, anyway?"

"Hey!" Cassie slammed her car into Park and hopped out, racing around the car to confront Ty. "I'm a damn good one!"

"Good? You call that little display back there good? By the way, your car—"

"Your dream is to open a pizza place. Giving up your dream is stressing you out. So I'm trying to help you grab your dream so you find happiness." Okay, she'd probably pushed him too hard. She had no choice now but to try to salvage it.

And then she'd fire herself before she could destroy anything else.

Ty glared at her, the glow from the streetlight casting spooky shadows over his face. "You know about my dream. You know I can't act on it. And then you flaunt that I can't have it. What kind of therapy is that?"

"It's the first step toward successful management of your stress." There had to be a way to make this work. She couldn't be an utter failure at her job as well as her personal life...could she? There'd be nothing left.

"You're wrong."

"No, I'm not." *I'm sorry, Ty!* What was that? Apologizing for upsetting a client? Since when did she feel bad when her clients got angry about their therapy? She'd made the right choice in bringing him here. Tonight had been required in order for him to heal. So what if he was irate and in denial?

Obviously, she was becoming soft. After that quality bonding time with Ty in the car, suddenly she couldn't handle him being mad at her? His anger was of no concern whatsoever and it didn't mean she'd made the wrong choice in bringing him here. Clients got mad at her all the time; it didn't mean she was an incompetent fool or that she should doubt herself.

Obviously, there was a little lesson here: never be friends with your clients. It made it too difficult to cause them pain.

Phew. She felt so much better now that she had sorted out the problem. It had been a little scary there for a moment when she'd thought she was a professional failure. Granted, she was pretty much recovered from the Drew fiasco, but her ego was a tiny bit shaky, and if her business fell apart...well, that might be a tad upsetting. Just a tad.

But it *wasn't* a problem because she *was* still a first-rate professional.

Ty glanced over her shoulder. "Your car is rolling down the street."

Yeah, right. As if she would fall for that little ploy. Recalcitrant clients never ceased to impress her with their creative attempts to escape from her penetrating therapy. The moment she turned her back on him to check out her car, he'd bolt to safety. Men were so transparent in the way they underestimated women. She was way too smart for him. Therapy would continue. "You said you'd never specifically mentioned your dream to Alexis. This should motivate you to do so."

He glared at her. "What kind of burden would that put on her? Asking her to choose between her need for stability and my dream? I won't do it."

"Maybe it's not a burden. Maybe it'll be a no-brainer for her." Cassie poked him in the chest. "Maybe you need to give her some credit. Maybe she's not some vulnerable little thing who needs your protection. Did that ever occur to you?"

Ty scowled at her. "She needs me."

"And what if she doesn't?" Cassie was cruising now. "Perhaps you're afraid to find out she doesn't."

"What?"

"Maybe you want to feel needed. Or maybe you're using Alexis as an excuse not to take a risk. But the problem really is with you being afraid."

Ty looked at her as if she'd told him to drive off a cliff. "I'll see you later." And then he turned and started walking again.

"Ty!" He couldn't leave. She was just starting to reach him.

He stopped and turned to face her. "What now?"

But he sounded weary, not angry.

"It's a little cold to walk all the way back to your place."

"I don't care."

"When I was little, my grandfather went hunting in Maine for a week and he got frostbite. The muscles on one side of his face got temporarily paralyzed. It took almost a month before his face went back to normal."

The corner of Ty's mouth curved up. "And you think that's going to happen me on the walk home?"

"It won't if you let me drive you home."

"First of all, you're a psychotic driver and I'd rather walk in the cold that risk my life. Second of all, you don't have a car to drive at the moment."

Fine. She'd call his bluff about the car. Cassie turned toward the street...and there was her car, meandering quietly along the flat road. "Huh. Look at that. Must've missed Park."

Ty flipped her a wry grin. "I don't lie."

This was certainly inconvenient. She had been on quite a roll and didn't want to abandon her quest just to rescue her car. So she wouldn't. It was a flat road. The car wouldn't pick up speed for at least another quarter of a mile. So she turned her back on it and faced Ty. "If you're going to marry her, you need to have more faith in her love for you."

"You aren't going to get the car?"

"Not at the moment." Cassie touched his shoulder. "Talk to her, Ty. Tell her how you feel. Break this cycle of playing the martyr."

Ty just shook his head in disbelief, then jumped off the curb and sprinted after her vehicle. "It isn't my relationship with Alexis that's making my blood pressure boil."

"I know. It's having to give up your dream." Cassie stood on the curb, raising her voice so he could hear her as he chased her car.

"You're wrong." He pulled open the driver's door.

"I'm never wrong." She followed him toward the car.

He dived into the front seat and slammed on the brakes. The car jerked to a stop with a healthy shudder as the four-wheel drive spiked the snowy road. He pushed open the passenger door. "Get in."

"You're driving?"

He just looked at her.

Okay, fine, so she hadn't exactly been at her best on the drive over. She'd be fine now that she was back to her usual collected self. "I'll drive my own car, thank you very much."

"Get in."

Or maybe she'd just slip into the passenger seat. After all, she had put him through a lot. A competent therapist always knew when to back off, and she was a damn good therapist. "Fine." She'd barely gotten the door shut when Ty started driving. "You know, I really do think you should be honest with Alexis."

Honesty was good. Just think how helpful it would have been in her relationship with Drew. *Sorry, Cassie, I have to sleep in the city because I'm going to be having sex all evening and it will be too late to drive home.* If he'd said that, then she could have taken an ax to all his furniture years ago and not even bothered with the whole "pay for the wedding and then cancel it and get none of your money back" fiasco.

"It's not Alexis. It's you."

"What's me?" Your true love? Your soul mate? Which would, of course, be a total shame, since she wasn't available for dating at the moment. Or ever.

"It's you who's driving me crazy. You're the one causing me to clench my jaw so hard that my whole head aches. You, my genius consultant, are the number one cause of my stress. Leave me alone."

"Ty..."

"Uh-uh." He held up his index finger to silence her.

"But..."

"No."

So the man needed some quiet time to contemplate the wonderful and insightful points she'd brought up tonight. She was astute enough to sense that and give him his space.

It certainly wasn't because a little part of her was desperately afraid she'd totally screwed everything up and deserved to have her tongue cut out before she did any more damage.

MISERABLE ROTTEN WEEK. Seven days had passed since she'd seen Ty. No phone call from him. No e-mail. He hated her. She'd pushed him too far and it was over.

And the fact she was feeling so miserably sorry for herself had absolutely nothing to do with the fact that two days ago had been Valentine's Day and she'd spent the evening in her office.

Not that Drew had been Mr. Romantic, but at least he would have ordered flowers or something. Good thing Ty wasn't with Alexis or Cassie would have *really* been upset. Or maybe that's why he hadn't called to schedule another therapy appointment. Maybe he'd flown out to visit Alexis for a surprise.

Cassie felt like she was going to be sick.

"How many days until his fiancée arrives?" Leo asked, interrupting a perfectly good misery session.

"I don't know."

Leo looked up from painting her toenails a seductive red in preparation for her Friday night date in less than an hour. "I thought she was arriving February eighteenth. That's Sunday."

"Sunday? No way." His fiancée was due back in two days? With Ty still unhealed? Cassie had failed. Great. So she failed at relationships and at her career. What a winner she was. She groaned and flopped back on the couch, burying her face in a pillow.

"I assume the groan of dismay is because Ty is even more stressed than he originally was, thanks to your intervention, and not because you still fantasize about him and he will be officially out of reach once she arrives and moves into his bed."

Into his bed. The thought made her—

No.

She would not torture herself.

But it really was nice of Leo to remind her about Ty and Alexis shacking up. As if it wasn't enough to already be worried about her utter failure as a therapist.

Not that she had to admit her personal feelings about Ty to herself or anyone else. She'd limit herself to professional worthlessness for now. "Of course I'm upset that he's still stressed." Her voice was muffled against the pillow. "I've never failed with a client before."

"It's not just that he's still stressed. You actually made him worse. Have you ever made someone worse before? This may be a first."

"Okay, so showing him the ice-cream shop may have been slightly premature. I still think it was the right thing to do." Cassie pulled the pillow off her face. It *had* been the right thing to do. She needed to believe that. Her timing had been a little off. That didn't mean she was a complete and utter incompetent. "I just need more time to follow through."

"You're out of time, girl. And you're out of chances. The man isn't going to open the door to you again."

"His house isn't even unpacked! What's Alexis going to think when she arrives and finds he hasn't unpacked in six months?" Alexis! *Dear God, please don't tell me I subconsciously sabotaged the mission because I wanted Alexis to reject him.*

Leo set the nail polish down and shot Cassie a concerned look. "You're getting way too emotionally invested in Ty. Residual baggage from Drew, I'm sure, but you need to shape up."

"Baggage from that scum? No way."

"Any woman who learns she trusted the wrong man for four years would be a little...wary. Battered, even. But for heaven's sake, don't latch on to Ty just because he's unavailable."

"You still think that's why I like Ty? As a friend, I mean?"

"As a friend. That's how you like him?"

"Of course. He's engaged." As he'd repeated frequently. Cassie wasn't a total idiot and she'd managed to pick up on that little fact. "He's smart and nice and he has a dream he's willing to put aside for the woman he lo...for the woman he's going to marry." And he wouldn't cheat on his fiancée.

Ty was a man his woman could trust.

There had to be a lesson in this somewhere that Cassie shouldn't judge the moral values of all the men in the world based on Drew's utter lack of ethics.

Or maybe not. She couldn't quite extrapolate Ty's values to the rest of the male population. Even if there were other men like him, what were the chances she'd find them? She was sure to fall in love with another two-timing loser and she really didn't need that.

Which was why she was going to buy lots of plants and talk to them instead of men.

"You actually like him." Leo sounded shocked. "And it's not because he's unavailable." She shook her head. "What are you doing, Cassie?"

"I don't like him. Not like that. He's engaged." Heaven help her if she was actually in love with Ty. That would be almost as stupid as marrying a man who slept with other woman on a regular basis, and she hadn't actually done that, so clearly she was above such poor decisions. "I mean, come on. I've had someone cheat on me. I'd never be a part of doing that to someone else." At least consciously. She'd better keep a close eye on her subconscious just to be sure.

"Then maybe you'd better increase your efforts to whip him into shape for Alexis. Don't you think?"

"You're right. You're absolutely right." Finishing Ty's therapy was the only way to prove she hadn't tried to screw him up on purpose. Abandoning him at this critical juncture *would* be a professional mistake and *could* smack of trying to interfere in his relationship with Alexis. Therefore, the only possible solution was for Cassie to pull her head out of the mud and march onward.

Two days left. She could totally do it...or she could at least try. "I'm going to deal with this situation. Now."

"Excellent." Leo held up a snack. "Want a chocolate caramel with imported toffee to fortify you? It's a new recipe, and those little worry lines are starting to contort your forehead. It's either chocolate or Botox if you want to attract any men."

"No thanks on the cellulite magnet. And the way my year is going, if I got a Botox injection, they'd miss and paralyze my face so I'd spend the next three months drooling. Not that that's a bad look for a single girl, but I just donated my box of handkerchiefs to charity, so I'd have nothing to clean up with." Cassie pulled on her boots and threw her arms into her parka sleeves. "Besides, I'm not going to date ever again, so it really doesn't matter how ugly and wrinkled I get."

Leo looked quite astonished. "You're turning down chocolate?"

"Sunday, Leo. I have until Sunday to earn my money. That's two days away."

Two days to ready him for his fiancée.

The hardest assignment Cassie had ever had.

She was not going to fail. No way. She simply wouldn't permit it. Which meant she had to take advantage of the forty-eight hours she had left. Starting now.

BY THE TIME Cassie reached Ty's house, it was almost nine o'clock.

Nine o'clock on a Friday night and she was going to work.

Yes, her social life was overflowing with interesting options now, wasn't it? Bummer.

Gah! She smacked her palm against her forehead. She wasn't interested in dating, remember? Being alone on Friday nights was her goal, her dream, her path toward never having her heart minced into tiny little pieces ever again.

So, it was a fabulous Friday night. Single, working, with no blinking lights on her answering machine. It was heaven, dammit, and she was going to love every minute of it even if it killed her.

Her footsteps crunching in the snow, Cassie climbed the steps to Ty's house, kicking at the chunks of snow on the edge of the walkway. There were lights on inside, so Ty was probably home.

Either that or at work. If it wasn't for his fiancée, he would be almost as much of a social outcast as she was.

Yeah, right. And gold would fall out of the sky the next time she sneezed. She definitely took the Dating Pariah Prize these days. She gritted her teeth. *And she loved every minute of it, remember?*

She rapped on the door and waited. A door slammed inside, and she heard Ty talking. To someone.

Cassie leaned closer to the door. His voice got louder as he neared her...and then she heard him use Alexis's name.

Alexis! Was she here already?

Yikes. No way was Cassie going to intrude upon their reunion.

For their sake.

It had nothing to do with tearing her own heart out of her body and throwing it on the ground for a good beating.

She whirled around to sprint back to her car...then heard the door open. "Cassie?"

Caught. She turned around. "I didn't realize Alexis was here...."

Ty was standing in the door, holding his phone to his ear, looking more than a little annoyed to see her. For the first time since she'd met him, he wasn't wear-

ing a suit. Faded jeans hung on his narrow hips, an old
gray sweatshirt encased his wide shoulders and a dark
field of stubble darkened his face.

Utterly masculine.

Deliciously rugged.

And he smelled like a mountain ranger. Woods and
spice with a hint of sophistication.

With friends like Ty, who needed a lover?

"Okay, so I'll talk to you next week," he said into the
phone, eyeing Cassie as if she were the angel of death.
"Bye." He disconnected and let the phone dangle from
his fingertips. "What are you doing here?"

"I'm sorry." Sorry? She hadn't come by to apologize.
She'd come by to treat him.

"For what?"

"For the ice-cream shop." Well, maybe her mind
hadn't come by to ask forgiveness, but her mouth apparently had other ideas. "I took the wrong approach."

"I don't believe you. You still think you did the right
thing."

See? Her mouth knew nothing. Running off and
apologizing without her permission and getting her
into trouble. Ty looked really annoyed that she hadn't
meant her apology. Didn't he understand? She *had* to
believe she'd done the right thing. Anything else
would send her catapulting off the precipice of despair. "I'm sorry I upset you."

"Are you? Or is it just part of the therapy? Some
steps are tougher to take and all that psychological
nonsense."

Darn it. He had her there, too, now that he pointed it
out. What was she sorry about? "I'm sorry you don't
trust me anymore."

Now, that was true.

Ty sighed. "It's not about trust. I just don't want to go down that path. We agree to disagree about what's best for me, and to go our separate ways."

"I can't do that."

"Why not?"

"Because you paid me to help you." And because she needed to prove to herself that she wasn't so screwed up that she was unable to do her job. And she did want him to be happy. He deserved it. And if being happy meant being with Alexis... Phew. This was a toughie. Try again. And if being happy meant being with Alexis, then she'd help...him...with...that...too....

Victory! She'd managed to complete that thought. Damn, she was a tough cookie.

"You tried. You earned your money. Move on."

"It's not just about the money." Hmm. Ty wasn't going to invite her in. It was going to be extremely difficult to heal him from the wrong side of a closed door.

"Professional pride?" he asked.

Okay, it was time to take control. She gave him a don't-mess-with-me look, pushed past him and walked down the hall toward the kitchen.

"Cassie!"

As if she would respond to that. She had two days to finish this assignment. Every minute counted.

She peeked in the living room on the way by. A fire in the fireplace. Nice. A good place to provide counseling, no? She walked in and sat down on the couch.

Ty appeared in the doorway and he didn't look pleased. Probably not used to having to share control of a situation. "I asked you to leave."

"And I ignored you. Could I have some water, please?"

Ty's eyes narrowed, and for a moment she thought

he might toss her over his shoulder and throw her out the front door. Then he gave a slight nod. "One drink. Five minutes. Then you leave."

"Fine." She had to at least sound reasonable.

"Five minutes," he repeated, before disappearing toward the kitchen.

The second he was out of sight, she closed her eyes and pressed her palms to her forehead. *Think, Cassie.*

How was she going to make amends for making Ty more of a stress case than he originally had been? Two days wasn't enough time to resolve the issues she'd brought up with the shop. She'd turned Ty into an angry and bitter man who was in no mood to woo a fiancée he hadn't seen in two years. Cassie needed to undo that damage and find another way to help him alleviate other causes of stress in his life. But how?

What was she thinking, showing up here without a plan? She never met with a client without a plan. The word *idiot* floated into her mind, but she refused to acknowledge it. She'd simply take stock of the room, and something here would prompt an idea. Roaring fire, so romantic...ahem. Ty's laptop was humming, a stack of files next to computer. Working on a Friday night. Hmm...

Had she been wrong? So busy trying to make his dreams come true that she'd lost sight of the more basic picture? That the man simply didn't know how to have fun? If he opened his pizza place, he'd work just as hard there. Alexis would never see him that way, either. Wow. How basic was that?

A genius Cassie was not.

She'd totally messed up.

Misdiagnosed the situation due to brain fog, no

doubt caused by the aftereffects of having her own dreams shattered.

Wait a sec. Was that what this was about? The fact that she wasn't married and on her way to having six kids and the perfect life?

She moaned and hugged her knees to her chin. *I give up.* No way to forge forward under the protective shield of delusions and self-accolades anymore. The ugly truth was that she was utterly and completed destroyed from the fiasco with Drew and she had no business existing, let alone trying to counsel anyone else.

Great. Admitting that really wasn't making her feel better. In fact, she wanted to crawl under Ty's couch and never move again. Just lie there, like an abandoned peanut butter sandwich, getting a good coat of mold, then becoming hard and crusty.

Dammit. Why couldn't she have kept up her delusions? The truth bit the big one.

"Tap water is all I have." Ty appeared in the doorway, his eyebrows furrowed in irritation. He held a glass of water.

"I'm so sorry, Ty."

"What now?" He set the glass on the coffee table, then returned to the doorway, a safe distance from her.

"I completely screwed up."

He folded his arms and leaned against the doorjamb. "You sound serious this time."

"I never should have taken you on as a client. I'm a disaster."

He cocked an eyebrow. "What kind of disaster?"

"Emotional. Professional. Whatever you guess, you'll be right." She rested her chin on her knees and stared numbly at the fire flickering in the stone hearth.

If she listened closely, she was quite sure the crackling of the flames was repeating the word *Loser*. No, that wasn't it. She listened more carefully. Aha. *Cassie is a loser*. Fire. Supposed to be so romantic and wonderful and it was ridiculing her.

She wondered if anyone else in history had been jeered by flames. Perhaps that was where that meaning of "roast" had come from. Ah, look at her. Even in the depths of misery, she could still think intellectually. Was she a keeper or what? What.

"I'm not following you." But some of the irritation had left his voice, so he sounded as if he only wanted to throw her down an icy slope instead of pulling off her toenails one by one and *then* throwing her down the icy slope.

"My dream. I lost it and I couldn't get it back. So I tried to make you live your dream." That was it. The truth. Out in the open. Freed to drill its way into her brain and make her never forget it.

The room was quiet, with no sound except the humming of Ty's computer and the flickering of the flames.

"Have you been drinking?"

"What?" She snapped her gaze to Ty. "What kind of a question is that?"

"One designed to stop you from feeling sorry for yourself. I like you better when you're feisty."

"Is this your way of rejecting my apology?"

"No." He levered himself away from the doorjamb and swung down beside her on the couch. "It's my way of telling you the apology doesn't suit you."

"What does that mean?"

Ty brushed her hair off her face, a smile curving his lips. "You're smart, independent and spunky. Sassy, even. That's what makes you special. You on my couch, talking about how some jerk took away your dreams and turned you into a professional incompetent... Well, it doesn't suit you."

"I apologize if it ruins your image of me, but I'm not always sassy, as you call it." She flopped on her back and clasped her hands over her head. Actually, now that she was fully committed to wallowing in her misery, it felt sort of good. "Leo's right. I'm still a mess from Drew. And until I shape up, I have no business trying to coach other people into a better space."

"Give it up, Cass."

She eyed him. "Why are you being unsympathetic? I had you pegged as the kind of man who doled out hugs whenever they were needed, without even being asked."

"That's what you need? A hug?"

"No. I just wanted a little sympathy. For you to accept my apology..." Her words were lost in the cotton of his sweatshirt as he grabbed her wrist, hauled her upright and wrapped his arms around her in the most powerful bear hug she'd ever experienced.

Safe.

Loved.

Protected.

It was as if Ty had created a bubble around her, fending off every negative vibe she generated.

By the time he released her, all the tension was gone from her body, leaving behind nothing but a limp pile of mush.

"Chocolate has no chance against that," she sighed. Okay, so maybe there was one reason not to completely write off men from her future. Hugs.

"What?"

"If you could bottle that hug and sell it, you'd be a

millionaire within days." It was a little annoying, though. He'd effectively managed to distract her from her sulk, which she had probably really needed. Come to think of it, maybe that was her problem. She hadn't committed nearly enough time to feeling truly sorry for herself. The weeks in the Bahamas didn't count because she'd been so busy trying to hate all the honeymooning couples.

A corner of Ty's mouth curved up. "I didn't realize a hug could do that much."

"Yours can." And it was annoying. Yanked her right out of her therapeutic pout.

"I think you're a first."

"I'm the first person you've ever hugged? What a complete waste." But she'd be more than happy to offer her services if he wanted to practice. For Alexis, of course.

"No, you're the first person to comment on my hugs."

"Then everyone else you've hugged must be..." Be what? How could anyone be immune to the feeling of Ty's muscular arms crushing her to his chest in a circle of safe comfort and...friendship? "Then they must have been dead. There's no other possible explanation."

Ty smiled and touched her cheek. "Or maybe you're just particularly susceptible."

She caught her breath, mesmerized by the feel of his fingertips against her skin. "Maybe..." Why, oh why, did this man have to be taken?

Ack! No! she didn't want him! The beast had kept her from feeling sorry for herself and acknowledging that she was every bit as screwed up and pathetic as she'd been pretending she wasn't. Who needed hugs like that?

Certainly not her.

9

CASSIE CARED ABOUT HIM. Ty knew, suddenly, with absolute certainty, that she would take care of him as much as he would look after her. Forever. They would make a team that could beat anything.... And he liked it.

Whoa.

He jerked his hands away from her and lurched to his feet, nearly staggering to keep his balance, while Cassie closed her eyes and pulled the pillow over her face, making some sort of squawk of frustration.

"You need a man."

She yanked the pillow off her face. *"What?"*

"A man. You need one." Ty grabbed his phone off the coffee table. There was only one way to stop himself from thinking about Cassie as more than a friend. Make her unavailable.

Because he didn't really want her for himself. It was just that he felt bad she was alone. So, if he could make sure she had someone else to love, then he wouldn't feel guilty for not being able to take care of her.

That's all it was.

Guilt.

Nothing else.

"Who are you calling?" Cassie sounded tense and more than a little hostile. That was fine. He owed her some unwelcome therapy, didn't he?

"A man worth trusting. That's what you need." And he knew just the one. "My brother."

"Your brother?" She sat up. "I'm not dating anyone, including your brother. Don't you see? I have to sulk for a while. It's part of the healing process and I totally messed up by depriving myself of it. I can't date and sulk at the same time."

"It's a brilliant idea. He's a great guy." Even as Ty punched the buttons on his phone, he wondered how in the hell he'd be able to stand Zach being with Cassie. What if they ended up together?

No, it would be good. Zach would take care of her.

His brother answered on the first ring. "Hello?"

"Zach. Got plans tonight?"

Cassie jumped up and tried to grab the phone, but Ty slung his arm around her and trapped her against his chest. Damn, she felt good wriggling against him. *Concentrate on Zach.* "I have someone I want you to meet."

"Who?" Zach asked. Ty could hear music playing in the background and knew Zach was working on Friday night, as he'd been doing for the last seven months.

"A woman. I think you'll like her. She's...cute." Cassie elbowed him in the stomach, socking all the air out of his gut. "Oomph."

"You okay, bro?"

"Fine." Ty tucked the phone against his shoulder and grabbed Cassie with his other arm, immobilizing her against his body. Damn. This felt way too good, but he couldn't exactly let go of her. "I think you'll love her." Words much harder to say than he'd anticipated, especially with his body responding to Cassie being wedged against him.

"Love? Now this I gotta see. Where do you want to meet?" Zach actually sounded relatively interested. Great. Ty was *so* pleased about this.

"Someplace casual," Ty said. "I'm going to spring this on her when I get off the phone and I'm not giving her time to go home and change. So pick a spot where jeans and hiking boots are acceptable. That's what she's wearing."

Zach snorted. "Jeans and hiking boots on a Friday night in the city?"

"Trust me. She looks hot in them."

Zach was quiet for a moment. "Maybe you should be the one taking her out tonight, bro."

"She's a friend, Zach. That's it. A friend who deserves a good guy."

Zach grunted skeptically, but said, "Fine. I'm in. Meet you at about ten-thirty?"

"Yep."

"I'll find a place and call you while you're on the road."

"Fine." Ty disconnected and released Cassie. She jumped away from him, a look of nervous terror on her face. "What's wrong?"

"A date? You want me to go on a date? I can't go on a date. I haven't been on a date since I was...like, twelve."

"Twelve? Since you've been with Drew for four years, that would make you sixteen now? I'd better call Zach back and tell him no bars."

She threw a pillow at him, which bounced off his toe and landed in front of the fireplace. "First of all, I don't need a pity date. Second, look at me. I can't go out on a date like this. I don't even have any makeup on. Third, I don't want a date. Didn't I just get done telling you I was still an emotional disaster from Drew? I need time to wallow in self-pity. Hadn't you noticed that I forgot to do that? Gross oversight on my part."

"The only way to heal is to get out there."

Cassie folded her arms across her chest and glared at him. "No. I want to feel sorry for myself."

"You have to go tonight."

"Why?"

"Because I care about you. As a friend." As if he was going to tell her it was for his sake, so he'd stop thinking of her as available. If she dated his brother, she'd be off-limits. Then Ty could focus on Alexis and the vows he would soon be making to her. "My brother is a super guy. You'll love him."

Vows. To Alexis.

He needed to make it feel right again.

"I don't have time for this," Cassie said.

"Time? It's nine o'clock on Friday night. What else do you have to do?"

"Fix you." Her eyes widened. "I totally forgot. That's why I'm here. To fix you."

"Fix me?" Ty groaned and ran his hands through his hair. At least she seemed to have gotten over her certainty that she was a total failure and shouldn't be trying to fix him. He supposed he should be glad.

"We have two days." She glanced at the room. "First, we'll unpack your house. Then...I'm going to have to teach you how to have fun."

"Two days? What happens in two days? Do you turn into a pumpkin?"

"I wish. That would make my life so much easier." Cassie stood up and walked over to a packing box that was still taped shut. "But no, in two days, Alexis arrives. I need to get you to the point where you don't work all the time. Train you to see the joy in other things besides work again." She sighed. "And *then* I'll have time to sulk and go for days without showering or getting out of my pajamas. I'll just have to put that on hold for now."

Ty frowned. "Alexis isn't coming on Sunday. She needs another couple weeks to wrap things up in Utah."

"Good." Cassie tore the tape off the box. "Good because we have more time. To work on your issues. That kind of good. Of course, it's not good that I'm going to have to put off sulking for another few weeks. But I can handle that. I'll just save up all my misery, get a good accumulation going, then deal with it all at once. Gives me time to go shopping for chocolate and frozen pizzas so I won't have to go out in public for months." She opened the box and lifted out a toilet brush. "I assume this goes in the bathroom?"

"I never should have accused you of not being tenacious."

"That's right. It's all your fault for questioning my professional tenaciousness." She pointed the brush at him. "Call your brother off. We have a mission to get this house cleaned up."

Ty folded his arms across his chest and took up residence against the wall. No matter how much he told himself he wanted to set up Cassie with Zach so it would eliminate the temptation, this date was also for her. Cassie needed help, the way she was trying to help him. He might not be a therapist, but he couldn't imagine that locking herself in her house and abandoning basic principles of hygiene for an extended period of time would be all that healthy for her psyche.

He could admit it: he cared about her. He wanted to

help her heal from the Drew debacle. But the way she needed to heal was to become emotionally involved with a man again. And Ty wasn't available to do it. No matter how much he wanted to…not that he would admit that little fact.

It simply meant he had to push as hard as necessary to help her. Even if it meant sacrificing his own sanity. For her, he'd do it. "Let's make a deal."

"I'm listening."

"You come meet Zach. Give him a chance. And I'll let you de-stress me. As long as you don't bring up the pizza place again." It wasn't a surrender as long as he maintained some control.

And to be honest, he did feel better when she was around. He hadn't realized how lonely his house was until she lit it up with her energy. Maybe he *had* been too focused on work. Maybe she had a point.

Cassie pursed her lips and rubbed her chin with the back of her hand. "I don't know. I really do have more important plans. Like unpacking your boxes and ordering several cases of tissues for my upcoming sulking episode."

"I swear you can trust him. Who would I know better than my own brother? Give life another chance, Cassie. You deserve it."

She studied him for a long moment, chewing her lower lip. Finally, she sighed. "If agreeing to this stupid bargain is the only way to reach you, then I have to do it. I may be a complete emotional and professional disaster, but that doesn't mean I'll abandon my client in the middle of therapy." She took a deep breath. "It's a deal. I'll go meet your brother."

"Great." Some victory. Ty felt like he'd been kicked in the gut by a bull on steroids.

DATING. MEN. She was going to be ill. No way was she ready for this.

Ty pulled open the door to the nightclub and Cassie knew she couldn't do it. She simply had to have her sulk-fest before she would be healthy enough to move on. And even then she wasn't making herself any promises. "I think I'm going to be sick. I'm going home."

"No. You need this." He put his hand on her back and propelled her through the doorway.

"Yeah, about as much as I need to have all my skin sanded off." Didn't the man have any compassion? And to think she'd been mooning over him, thinking he was this wonderful, doting guy. He was an autocratic jerk and she hated him.

His hand tight around her arm, he pulled her into the crowded bar, which was dark and loud. And claustrophobic. Women were wearing sexy silk outfits, high heels and expensive jewelry. Men were in slick black jackets and shiny white shirts, flashing gold watches and stylish haircuts. "Um...Ty? I'm not dressed for this. Let's do this another night when I can prepare. Like tomorrow night? I promise I'll come." Yeah, right. She'd be hiding in the crawl space under her house when Ty came to pick her up. Rodent droppings, cobwebs and nasty bugs would be far preferable to facing the singles scene in New York City.

For heaven's sake, she was supposed to a dowdy married woman by now. Not competing with all the flesh-showing hotties.

"There's Zach."

"Great." No escape now. "I really think I'm going to throw up." Her skin felt cold and hot at the same time.

Ty stopped suddenly and grabbed her shoulders, turning her toward him. "Cassie, look at me."

She obeyed, fixating on the face of the one man she actually trusted. Obviously a poor choice given that he'd abused her trust by dragging her to this bar.

"You can have faith in Zach. He'd never treat you badly. I would know, wouldn't I? With him being my brother and all?"

"I don't know. Maybe you haven't seen him in twenty years."

"Do you trust me, Cass?"

"Yes." But that was only because her brain wasn't functioning at the moment. As soon as she got through her pity parade, she'd be thinking much more clearly.

"Then know I wouldn't introduce you to Zach if I thought there was any chance of him treating you badly. He's a good guy." Ty grinned. "He's like me. Only younger and better looking. Or at least, that's what the women all say. Plus he's more fun. You'd like that, wouldn't you? A man who actually knew how to have fun?"

"You'll be fun, too, by the time I'm through with you."

"It's already working."

"Yeah, you're a real barrel of laughs. Obviously, I'm a raging success."

"I haven't spent a Friday night away from my computer in years. Just think. By coming here and meeting Zach, you're already working your magic on me."

Really? So, by having him focus on her misery, she was healing him? Not that that changed the fact she was stuck with a *date*. "Don't try to distract me."

"Why not? It's working. Your face actually has more color than a sheet of ice." Before she could react, he dropped a quick kiss on her forehead, then spun her back toward the corner. "Let's take advantage before you remember why you're panicking."

As if she could possibly remember anything while her forehead still burned from his kiss.

What she really needed was to go home, curl up in her bed and moan. For several months.

How in the world was she going to get through tonight?

TY SAW THE MASCULINE appreciation in Zach's eyes the instant his brother saw Cassie.

And for the first time in his life, Ty wanted to punch his little brother.

Instead, he directed Cassie toward the table. "Zach, this is Cassie Halloway. Cass, this is my little brother, Zach."

"Not so little anymore," Zach said, rising to his feet with a smile that was much too warm and friendly. "Great to meet you, Cassie."

"Hi." Cassie shook Zach's hand and Ty noticed that his brother let his fingers grip Cassie's longer than necessary.

Which was perfect. Zach liked Cassie, just as Ty had thought he would. And Ty was going to be just fine with it. "Have a seat, Cass."

Cassie chose the bench opposite the one Zach had been sitting in, sliding across the red vinyl with awkward hesitation.

"Sit..." But before he could direct Zach into the same side of the booth Cassie was sitting on, Zach returned to his original side. Across from Cassie.

Which meant Ty had to sit next to Zach or beside Cassie.

Or excuse himself and go out to the alley and beat up some trash cans. Which he wouldn't mind doing. The sight of Cassie and Zach across from each other was a little harder to take than he'd anticipated.

But he'd get over it.

"Sit here." Cassie patted the seat beside her, eyebrows knitted in nervousness, her cheeks still pale. "Please."

As if he could turn down that request. Ty swung into the booth beside Cassie, throwing his arm casually across the back of the bench. For support. As a friend.

CASSIE SHIFTED NERVOUSLY in the seat, trying to concentrate on what Zach was saying. His coloring was the same as Ty's, his mannerisms similar, his looks more classic and perfect.

She liked Ty's rugged masculinity better.

So what?

She had to get over it. It was merely self-defense, because she wasn't ready to date. No man would meet her standards, because if he did, she'd have to date and there was no way she was going to start with that just yet. Or ever.

But she had to get through tonight without making a total idiot of herself. Tonight was all about healing Ty. For Ty, she could get through this. Because she was the best damn stress therapist there was.

Armed with renewed resolve, she leaned forward and tried to tune in to Zach. He was asking her a question.... Oh. How she knew Ty. "He hired me to de-stress him."

"Really?" Zach looked amused and she realized he had a nice smile. Warm. Look at how healthy she was! Noticing a man had a nice smile. "Never thought the

day would come when my brother actually acknowledged that he's a psycho."

"I bet Cassie could help you out, too," Ty said.

"I agree," Zach said, his tone just a little too mean-
ingful for Cassie's comfort.

Okay, so Zach thought she was attractive. What was
wrong with that? He was a nice guy, good-looking,
personable. What more could she ask for?

"So, do you want to dance?" Zach asked.

"Dance?" But it was a slow song. She hadn't been
held by a man other than Drew in forever—not counting Ty, of course. For the sake of her job, she could handle conversation and even notice that he was decent
looking, but a dance? His hands on her body? "I..."

"Come on." Zach stood up and held out his hand. "I
won't bite."

She couldn't do this. *Deep breath, Cassie. It's not a big
deal.* A dance. It didn't mean anything at all. Just part of
her therapy for Ty. She could do it.

"Go ahead, Cassie. It'll be fun," Ty said.

She looked at Ty and the determination on his face
that she be with his brother. He wanted her with Zach.
Ty didn't want her. Yes, she knew he was engaged to
Alexis. Yes, she knew nothing could happen between
them. But that didn't stop her from feeling just a little
bit hurt. And disappointed.

Which was ridiculous. She didn't need him or even
want him. She could handle another man just fine and
she didn't need to lean on Ty. Cassie took a deep
breath and smiled at Zach. "Yes, I'll dance with you."

Mumbling something unintelligible, Ty slid off the
bench and out of her way, leaving an open path toward
the dance floor. But he wouldn't look at her, not even
to give her a boost of self-confidence. His eyes were

fixed across the room, his back turned slightly toward her.

She was on her own.

Cassie lifted her leaden hand and set it in Zach's. He smiled and tightened his grip, leading her onto the dance floor...away from Ty...away from safety.

To her relief, he stopped on the edge of the floor, only twenty feet from Ty, who had returned to the booth and was staring into the beer Zach had been drinking, his hands wrapped around the bottle. He looked so alone.

Zach slipped his arms around her and pulled her up against him.

Instinctively, Cassie stiffened, stopping before their bodies could touch. This was too weird. He was a stranger and he was holding her. Was this what dating was all about? Having men she didn't know touch her?

Of course it was. It was normal and fine. *Get a grip, Cassie.*

She rested her hands on his shoulders...well, more on his chest, as if she were planning to block him if he moved too close.

Which she was.

"Relax, Cassie," Zach said. "I swear I won't attack you."

Perceptive. Just like his brother. Cassie managed a small smile. "It's just that this is my first venture into the dating world after being in a long relationship."

"Mine, too."

"Really?"

Zach nodded. "I dated a woman for seven years. We broke up last summer and I've been avoiding the dating scene ever since. 'Til tonight. Ty has never wanted me to meet a woman before, so I figured he had to think you were pretty special."

"Really? You think Ty thinks I'm special?"

Zach cocked his head. "Yes, I do."

Warmth bubbled through her and she felt herself relax. Not that she cared if Ty thought she was special. It just meant that he didn't hate her for the pizza place thing. And she didn't care about that, either. Why would she care what Ty thought of her? Just because he was kind, loyal and supportive didn't mean she had any feelings for him whatsoever.

"See? Nothing to worry about," Zach said.

She immediately tensed up again and saw from the tightness around Zach's mouth that he noticed, as well. How could he not? It was a good thing she wasn't interested in ever securing a man's interest again, because being a frigid ice queen really wouldn't be the way to do it.

"So...what do you think of Ty?" Zach asked.

"Great guy. A little serious, but he's funny and warm and devoted.... He was worried about me? Can you imagine? That's why he wanted us to meet, because he knew I was afraid to date again and he swears you're a good person."

Zach continued to sway to the music, but he didn't look as if he was listening to it. "You guys have become friends, huh?"

"I guess."

Conversation faded into awkward silence and Cassie let her gaze drift back to their booth. Ty was watching them, a dark scowl on his face, his hands still clenched around Zach's beer.

Her heart tightened and she nearly told Zach to let her go so she could go check on Ty. As a client, of course. She had to make sure the therapy was working, not hurting. She compromised by nudging Zach and nodding toward Ty. "You think he's all right?"

Zach twisted around to glance at Ty, then looked back at her, a thoughtful look on his face. "I'm beginning to wonder...."

"I'm sure he's fine," Cassie said firmly, nodding for emphasis. "And I'll check when we finish dancing. Just to see if it's stress. Because that's my job, you know."

Zach stared at her for a long moment, until Cassie began to squirm under his probing gaze. "What?" she finally asked.

"Hang on a sec," Zach said. He beckoned to Ty, who shook his head and glowered at them.

He gestured again and Ty got to his feet, slamming the beer into the tabletop. He stalked across the floor. "Yeah?"

"Dance with Cassie for a second."

Her heart fluttered even as Ty's face grew darker. "Why?"

"I have to make a call."

"A call? To who?"

"I'll be back in a sec." Zach peeled Cassie's hands off his shoulders and wrapped them around Ty's neck. "Dance."

And then he was gone.

"You don't have to dance with me," Cassie said quickly.

But Ty was already wrapping his hands around her waist and pulling her up against him. "Are you having fun with Zach?"

Now *this* felt right. Not scary, not awkward. Cassie sighed and snuggled against him, resting her cheek against his chest. "He's a nice guy."

"Good."

"But…" She could feel his heart thudding in his chest. "I—I don't know. It's just…there's no magic." Ty's familiar scent wafted through the air. So comforting, so safe. Ty would never hurt her. Ever. With him, she'd be able to relax and trust.

His hands tightened on her, spanning her lower back and pulling her closer. "Maybe you need to give it more time. I sort of threw Zach on you."

"You think that's it?"

"Could be."

"Maybe I'm not ready for dating. I couldn't even let my body touch his."

"I noticed."

She didn't seem to be having the same reservations dancing with Ty. Her body was pressed up against his, the heat from his chest warming her to her toes. Her belly was starting to do an interesting little dance. She was beginning to feel really warm. Tingles were going down her spine and she had goose bumps on her arms. Uh-oh. This couldn't be good. "Um…Ty?"

"Mmm?"

"Do you think we're dancing a little close?"

"It's because there's no pressure between us," he said, his voice muffled by her hair. "Because we're just friends."

"Really?" She buried her face in his sweatshirt, breathing in the distinctive scent that was only his. So this was what it was like to dance with a friend? Funny how it felt almost the same as dancing with someone who she was so wildly attracted to that she could barely keep from dragging him off to a corner and attacking him.

"It has to be," he added.

He was right. They had no other choice, no other options. Friends. No more. "Then I'm glad we're friends." The fact that she was suddenly recalling their one kiss with perfect clarity, knew exactly what his lips felt like against hers, what he tasted like, how his breath felt on her face, was not an indication that she had suddenly taken the friends thing way too far.

"I'm not." He took one hand off her back and smoothed her hair off her face, his fingers tangling in the loose strands. "I wish we'd never met."

"But...why?" She attempted to step away from him, trying to close her heart against the pain that instantly swelled.

"Oh, don't be ridiculous. Come back here." He grabbed her around the waist and hauled her back against him, anchoring her against his rock-hard body. "You've stalked me, dragged me away from my work on repeated occasions and tortured me by waving my dreams in front of my face. You have to admit it hasn't exactly been a pleasure cruise."

But he was grinning.

"You're not mad." Thank heavens. She felt so much better. Except for the fact that she was unable to drum up an acceptable explanation for the goose bumps and the tingles she still had.

"Of course I'm mad," he said. "That's why I want to set you up with Zach. I figure if I can get you to start interfering in his life, then I'll be a free man."

Cassie lifted her chin, returning the grin. "I have plenty of room in my life to stalk more than one stubborn client." Just because she'd finally realized she was sexually obsessed with him didn't mean she couldn't joke with him.

"So, even if you started climbing my brother's fire

escape in the middle of the night, you'd still be at my house in the morning armed with your latest insane scheme?"

"Yes, and my schemes aren't insane. They are all part of my carefully orchestrated plan to heal you."

Ty spun her around, holding her tight. "So, are you going to start climbing through my brother's window in the middle of the night?"

The easy answer was "no." Though Zach was a nice enough guy, he didn't suck her into his soul the way Ty did.

But soon Ty would be occupied by Alexis, and Cassie would have to forget about him. Perhaps Zach would be the best answer in order to find the strength to move on...assuming the upcoming weeks of mourning didn't solve the problem. "Maybe I will see Zach again. If he asks."

Ty pursed his lips and nodded tersely. "Good."

"So...if I ended up dating your brother...we could spend holidays with you and Alexis?" How torturous did that sound? Watching Ty with another woman? Because, now that Cassie had acknowledged that she had the hots for Ty, she wasn't sure that hanging out with him and Alexis would occupy the top spot on her list of preferred activities.

Ty grimaced. "Sounds perfect. Song's over. Let's go."

He guided her back to the table, where Zach was sprawled, his beer bottle dangling loosely in one hand. "You two look good together," he said.

"Cassie would look good with anyone," Ty muttered, dropping down in the booth. He propped his feet up on the bench, taking up the entire seat.

The only place for Cassie was next to Zach. No problem. If she was going to start dating him, she'd have to be able to sit next to him, right? So she'd just slide in there next to him and... Whoops. What was that? Nature calling? Too bad. She'd have to postpone the intimate moment. "I have to go to the ladies' room. I'll be back in a minute."

There was nothing like a women's bathroom to hide from men. And that's what she was doing until she managed to forget about the feel of Ty's body against hers and how it made her go all zingy. Zach was a good guy and he deserved a chance. She deserved a chance, too, actually. If she could never get past Ty—and Drew, for that matter—she'd wind up bitter and alone with serious hygiene problems.

And the truth was, she didn't really want to end up alone.

There. She'd admitted it. That had to be a good first step, right?

So...what was the next step? Having random sex with a bunch of strangers until she was comfortable dating again? Fantasize about Ty until she'd had her fill of him?

Somehow, neither of those seemed to be particularly fabulous options. So what in the heck was she supposed to do?

10

TY WATCHED CASSIE RUN across the floor, dodging people and ducking elbows. Something had freaked her, and it was all he could do not to jump up and sprint after her, collaring her until she told him what was wrong.

"You going to go after her?" Zach asked.

"No. She'll be all right." Wouldn't she? Maybe he should check on her. Make sure she was all right. Maybe she needed another hug or something....

"So..." Zach leaned on the table, sliding his beer from hand to hand across the slick surface. "How's Alexis?"

Ty scowled. "Fine."

"When is she moving here?"

"A couple weeks."

Zach nodded. "You psyched?"

"Psyched? I don't know."

"Wrong answer, bro."

Ty snagged a beer from a passing waitress. "How can that be a wrong answer?"

"Your fiancée is about to move in with you after living in another state for the last six years, two of which you've been engaged. You should be flipping out with excitement."

"I'm beside myself with glee."

"Yeah, it shows." Zach took a long sip of his beer. "Cassie seems nice."

"She's great."

"So, Alexis is fine and Cassie is great."

Ty twisted the cap off and flipped it across the table at his brother. "What's your point?"

"Do you love her?"

"Alexis?"

"Either of them."

"Them?"

"Cassie or Alexis?"

"I'm marrying Alexis."

"That's not what I asked you."

Ty glared at his brother. "I brought Cassie here to meet you, didn't I?"

"That's what you said."

"What are you trying to say? That I love Cassie and should be marrying her?"

Zach held up his hands. "I didn't say that."

"Well, it's not true. I'll never abandon Alexis. She's alone in this world and she needs stability. And I'll give it to her. So back off and quit trying to make trouble where there isn't any!"

"Chill out, big brother. I was just testing the waters."

"For what? Piranhas?" Ty took a deep breath and tried to relax into the booth. He didn't love Cassie. What a stupid notion.

"I want to get Cassie's number, but first I want to make sure you'd be cool with it."

"Of course I'm cool with it," Ty snapped. "That was the point of tonight, wasn't it?"

Zach raised his eyebrows. "Let go."

"Of what?"

"Cassie."

"What does that mean?"

"You're being overprotective. You've introduced us, now let it happen. Let her go, Ty. She isn't yours."

She isn't yours. The words burned their way into Ty's brain, the pain not even relieved when he pressed the cold beer bottle against his forehead. Zach was right. Cassie wasn't his. Alexis was his. He belonged to Alexis. Cassie deserved Zach. She didn't need Ty scowling and being nasty just because he felt protective of her.

Because that's all it was. Overprotectiveness for a vulnerable friend.

This was going to be a long night.

TY WAS STILL ASLEEP when the doorbell jerked him awake Saturday morning. Yanked him out of a nightmare in which he was at Zach and Cassie's wedding as best man. A rabid dog had just bitten Zach on the leg, prompting a 911 call and a postponement of the wedding.

Ty always liked dogs.

The doorbell rang again, followed by someone pounding on the door.

Better the door than returning to sleep and revisiting Zach and Cassie's wedding.

Ty swung his feet out of the bed, landing with a thump on the carpet. Beige. Would Alexis keep the beige carpet?

As if he cared. It was just a house.

He yanked on a pair of sweats, then jogged down the steps, flipping the heat up to a decent daytime temperature. He flicked the lock on the door, then pulled it open...and suddenly he didn't feel cold anymore. Angry, bitter and hostile. But not cold. "Hi, Cassie."

Her mouth opened, her full lips parted, but no sound came out. And she was staring at his chest.

Nice, Ty. Always good to open the door clad in nothing but a pair of sweats. Especially when the woman gawking at you had the power to make your body spring to attention in the most inappropriate of ways.

Growling, Ty spun away from the door, leaving Cassie on the front step. She could come in if she wanted. Or not.

Preferably not.

But when he heard her boots thud in his front hall and the door close, he was pleased. She'd come in. He immediately scowled. *Pleased?* Was he insane? He didn't care about her, didn't care if she ever appeared in his house again and certainly didn't care if she married his brother.

"Ty?"

"What?" He stalked into the living room and found a sweater on the floor. He tugged it over his head, shielding his body from her inspection. Only then did he turn to face her. "Why are you here? I would've thought you'd be sleeping in, dreaming about Zach."

"I wish I could dream about him." She tugged her stocking cap off, tossed her mittens on his couch and unzipped her parka.

"You didn't dream about him? That's too bad. Because you two belong together." And he'd keep repeating it until he could say it without wanting to choke Zach.

"Do we?"

"Absolutely. So you should be dreaming about him." Nope, still wanted to do some permanent damage to his brother. Needed a little more practice.

"Actually, I didn't sleep much."

"Why not?"

"Mental breakdown from being forced onto the dating scene before I was ready." She shrugged off her coat and dropped it on his couch. "Ready?"

"For what?"

"Unpacking."

Ty groaned. Spending the day engaged in domestic endeavors with Cassie was definitely not conducive to forgetting how good she felt in his arms. "I need to work."

"Not today."

"I have clients depending on me."

"And you have a fiancée who doesn't deserve to live like this. You promised you'd let me treat you, remember? That was the deal we made last night."

Damn. She had him there. He'd never go back on his word. "Can we start tomorrow, at least? I really need to work." There was no way in hell he could stand being around her today. Not when he could still recall how she felt in his arms on the dance floor. He needed some distance. Now.

"No worries. I'll unpack by myself." Cassie marched over to the box she'd opened last night and pulled out a furry kangaroo. "Alexis's?"

"Um...that's mine."

She grinned. "You have a stuffed kangaroo?"

"From when I was a kid." He walked over and tried to snatch it from her, but she ducked under his arm and danced around to the other side of the coffee table.

"What's his name?"

"Harvey."

"That has to be the cutest thing I've ever heard. A big, strong, handsome guy keeping a stuffed kangaroo named Harvey."

"Handsome?" She thought he was handsome?

Cassie's cheeks immediately flushed and she tossed Harvey at him. "Or it's the sign of a wimp who couldn't protect his woman from a stiff breeze, let alone any real threat of danger."

"I'll always protect my woman."

Cassie smiled. "Yeah, I'm getting that picture. Ever occur to you that today's woman might not want to be protected all the time?"

"Ever occur to you that maybe you're trying to be too tough and that maybe you'd feel better if you actually let someone take care of you?

Cassie's smiled faded. "Don't judge me."

"You think I'm right, don't you?"

She turned away and pulled a pair of hockey skates out of the box. "You skate?"

"Used to play hockey in college."

"Hmm." She set the skates on the floor and returned to the box.

"Cassie, stop." Ty walked over and caught her wrist. "You can't unpack my house while I work."

She stopped and eyed his hand, which was still wrapped around her arm. "Why not?"

He released her. "Because I'll feel...weird." *And because I'll just sit back and watch you, fantasizing about what it would be like if you lived here. With me.* Ty groaned. Was he a mess or what? Obviously, his brilliant plan with Zach had failed. Not only was he still thinking about her, but now he was also jealous of his brother. "Did Zach call you yet?"

She blinked. "It's only eight in the morning."

"So, is that a 'No?'"

"Of course it's a no."

"If he calls, are you going to go out with him?" What

did he think he was going to accomplish with this line of questioning? Torturing himself? No. He just needed to know she was interested in someone else. Then he'd be able to move on. Or at least he'd better.

Cassie sighed and rubbed the back of her hand against her chin. "I suppose I'll go on a date or two with him. If he calls."

"Good." Ty was clenching his teeth so hard he thought they were going to crack. "So, why don't you leave my house then?"

"Leave? Why?"

"I'll unpack and you can come back tonight and inspect. How's that?"

Cassie tilted her head and studied him. "Do you have a problem with me dating Zach?"

"No. I'm happy for both of you." Ty walked over to the box and yanked out a hockey puck. Hmm...if he threw it through his window, the tinkling melody of shattering glass might make him feel better. Then again, he did own the house and would have to pay for the repairs, so maybe he needed to rethink that particular course of action.

"Well, I could use a little support," she said.

As if he could do that. "I did my job. You're on your own now."

Cassie turned toward him, and that's when he saw the vulnerability in her eyes. "Don't you get it, Ty? I'm scared. I don't want to be out there dating again, but I have to be. You're the only man I trust, and I need your support. You're the one who made me get out there, so you can't abandon me now."

Ty tore his eyes away from her and gazed at the ceiling. "I can't be your best friend."

"Just a friend, Ty."

"Can't."

"Why not?"

Because I want more than your friendship.

Hell.

The thought was out of its prison. And freedom gave it strength and power that was unwelcome and dangerous. Only solution? Get Cassie out of his life. "I think you should leave."

"But..."

"I'll work on unpacking today. I'll even turn the music on and dance a little bit. Learn how to have fun again. You're doing your job. Okay?"

She looked so vulnerable, as though she was hovering on a tightrope and the slightest wind could make her tumble off. He steeled his heart. "Go, Cassie. I'll follow your instructions. Just leave." His voice was harsher than he intended, but it worked, for she grabbed her coat off the coach and walked out without another word.

The front door slammed and then the house was silent.

Ominously silent.

Lonely.

Empty.

Except for her stocking cap and mittens, which still lay on the couch. Abandoned. Ty picked up the hat and held it to his face. It smelled like Cassie. Pure, feminine and alluring.

He cursed and threw it back on the couch.

He'd start upstairs.

SHE'D BEEN TO THE GROCERY store and stocked her freezer. She'd done all her laundry. Bought lots of tissues and showered. She'd made her decision and she was ready. It was time for a top-of-the-line, no-luxury-forgone, old-fashioned pity party. By the time she emerged from her cocoon of misery, she'd be ready to become a dating fiend and she'd give Zach the first opportunity. Or so she hoped. It would be a major bummer to disappear into a vat of tears and mourning for several months, only to emerge just as broken as she'd begun.

But it was worth trying. She had no idea what else to do.

Sure, she'd been planning to heal Ty first. But he didn't want her help. She wasn't going to fight him any longer.

She counted the frozen pizzas in her freezer. Forty-two. A few more would have been good, but there was no more room.

"Are you opening a pizza place or something?" Leo asked.

Cassie yelped and jumped, smacking her head on the freezer door. "Good God, Leo! What are you doing? You scared the hell out of me!"

Her friend held up a key. "You didn't answer the door."

"Maybe because I don't want company." Cassie shut the freezer. "What do you want?"

Leo eyed her. "I want to know what's up with all the pizza, why you're wearing those hideous old sweatpants and when was the last time you showered."

"I'm going to have a pity party, they're comfortable and this morning, but I didn't do my hair. Any more questions before I kick you out so I can feel sorry for myself?"

Leo sat down at the kitchen table. "This is all about Ty and Alexis?"

That was definitely a post-pity-party topic. Cassie didn't have the capacity to discuss the coupling of Alexis and Ty just yet.

"You love him, don't you?"

"No!" Oh, who was she kidding? She sighed and sat down on the floor, leaning against a kitchen cabinet. "It's getting way too complicated with Ty. He hates me."

Leo rolled her eyes. "Self-pity isn't attractive."

"It's not self-pity. It's true."

"Are you listening to yourself? So what if he hates you? Don't all your clients hate you at some point?"

"Yes, but..." Cassie hesitated. "It's also... Well...I'm really not recovered from this whole wedding thing. I need time for myself." To cry and moan and feel really sorry for herself, to be precise.

"About time you realized it. Maybe now you can finally deal with it and move on."

Where was the sympathy? The pity? The love? "It was a very traumatic experience for me."

"Of course it was." Leo patted Cassie's arm. "So you see? It's not Ty, after all. It's always been Drew. So you can keep treating Ty."

"Um...there's something else."

Leo lifted a brow. "What?"

"I—I think I'm starting to...have feelings for him." There. It was out. The whole truth. She was upset that Ty hated her, she wasn't over the marriage thing and she liked Ty.

If it weren't such a totally abominable situation, it would almost be laughable how badly she'd messed everything up. "And I have to go up to my room and wallow in misery for at least a couple of months. I haven't done that, and I think that's why I'm such a disaster. I can't heal Ty and cry all day, too, so I have to choose."

Leo whapped Cassie on side of her head with her palm.

"Ow!" She pressed her hand to her head. "What was that for?"

"Feeling sorry for yourself. I can't stand that. Make other women proud. Or better yet, make yourself proud."

"Myself?"

"Yes. Show that you can get on with your life after almost marrying a jerk. Earn your money and move on."

"But..."

"And so what if you like Ty? He's a good guy and he's worth liking. Hot, too. It's healthy that you're noticing other men. It's about time."

"But he's engaged...."

"Oh, give me a break, Cassie. From what you've said, he's so moral that he'd never abandon Alexis for a fling. You aren't going to break them up. So don't worry about that. Just suck it up and get on with your own life."

Dammit! Cassie didn't want to get on with her life! She wanted to feel sorry for herself. "It's not that easy."

"Of course it's not easy. That's why there are people like you making a profit from other people's misery."

"That's not what I do." That sounded horrid. "I help people."

"Then help yourself."

"I am. That's why I need to go up to my room and..."

"Tell me something, Cassie. If you give up on your

life for a few months to be miserable, aren't you letting Drew win?"

Drew was a bastard who didn't deserve to win at anything.

"Just think. While you're sitting in your room, you don't earn any income. Then you'll have to sell your house. And poor Ty will have to go through the rest of his life stressed out because you wouldn't finish helping him. How does all that make Drew suffer for betraying you? I think the best punishment is to show him that you're glad you didn't get stuck with him."

"Well, I *am* thankful I didn't marry him. It's just that the way it happened wasn't exactly wonderfully therapeutic, you know?" Gah. She'd been trying to survive for so many weeks when everyone kept insisting she must be so upset, and now that she was finally ready to admit she was devastated, no one would let her sulk. Bunch of heartless cads they all were.

"Tell you what. I'll make a deal. Finish this thing with Ty. Then, if you aren't feeling better about yourself, I'll bring you food for two months so you never have to leave your house."

"Really?" Wow. Two months without even having to set foot outside her house. People would envy that pity session. Maybe she could even deduct business expenses as research for future clients. Maybe others would benefit from being locked in their bedroom for several months. "That's not a bad deal."

"There you go. Stick it out with Ty for two more weeks. But you have to really try to help him. It doesn't count if you drive by his house six times and never stop."

"And what about the dreams I'm starting to have about him when I sleep?"

Leo grinned. "Enjoy them. Every woman needs a fantasy man."

"Really?" So maybe that's what she'd been doing wrong her whole life. Not having fantasies. "And you don't think I should feel guilty lusting after a man who's engaged to someone else?"

"Nah." Leo cocked an eyebrow. "Unless you showed up at his house clad only in your lingerie. But then you'd have your professional ethics to deal with as well."

"Good point." Cassie flexed her fingers. She could do this. Survive two more weeks before she dropped out of society. And honestly, it would be good to finish this. She'd never admitted defeat with a client yet. And if she gave up on Ty, she'd have to have new brochures printed up that didn't claim a perfect track record, and who wanted to do that? She nodded. "Okay. I can do this. It's not that long."

How hard could it be to endure another few days?

Piece of cake. "And if I heal him before Alexis arrives, do I get to start my mourning period earlier?"

Leo patted her knee. "You show me a relaxed, happy Ty and you're free."

Well, all right. There was incentive! Cassie would get right on it. Ty would have no chance against her brilliant tactics.

THIRTY MINUTES LATER, Cassie was at Ty's house, dressed in her warmest clothes, a stocking cap artfully worn to hide the bad-hair day. She banged on the door. Ruthlessly. Powerfully. Forcefully.

Because she was a woman to be reckoned with.

After several minutes, Ty opened the door. The instant he saw her, he sighed and leaned on the frame. "Has anyone ever called you a stalker?"

"Shut up." She didn't have time for this. She was on a mission.

He blinked. "What?"

"Quit bellyaching, get your parka on and grab your skates." If it was okay to fantasize about him, then was it permissible to notice how broad his shoulders were? Maybe, but she still felt awkward. He was someone else's fiancé, after all.

"Now?"

"Of course now. Why do you think I'm here?" Yeesh. Men could be so dense.

"But I'm unpacking."

"As if the boxes are going to run away while you're gone." She pulled up her sleeve and looked at her watch. "I'm timing you. Thirty seconds or..."

"Back to the old Cassie, huh?" He raised an eyebrow, some of his irritation fading, replaced with amused respect.

"Older, wiser and much more cynical. You're down to fifteen seconds."

Ty grinned, the same devastating grin that had caught her attention that first night at the dance.

"Twelve seconds," she snapped.

"Bump it back up to ninety seconds, agree to take my car and I'll come."

"Eighty-five seconds and why your car?"

"Because I've seen you drive."

"Oh." That had been one of the less brilliant moments of her career.

"Eighty-eight seconds and my car?" he suggested.

"Fine. But only because I'm feeling indulgent today."

"I'm the one feeling indulgent. Putting up with another one of your therapy attempts isn't exactly my number-one fantasy."

"Every girl loves to hear she isn't a man's fantasy. I appreciate the compliment." Cassie looked at her watch. "You're down to seventy-six seconds. Better stop the idle chitchat or you're in violation of our oral contract."

"What's the penalty for breach of contract?"

"One hundred continuous hours of stress management therapy with me."

"Sounds like cruel and unusual punishment."

"Sixty-eight seconds."

"The instinct for self-preservation prevails. I'll be ready in thirty."

11

COULD SHE POSSIBLY have chosen a stupider activity? Perhaps she'd been a mite hasty in planning this session, forgetting she had zero skating ability.

Oh, who was she kidding? She hadn't planned it all, just grabbed her skates and run over to his house without any forethought whatsoever. What an excellent idea. Having a treatment plan wasn't working, so abandon all protocol and wing it? Yeah, good one. Not.

It was official. She was terrible at her job.

"Get up, Cassie," Ty chuckled.

"No." She let her head drop back against the ice of the frozen pond, every inch of her body bruised, aching and cold. "Leave me here to die, please."

"We've been here for less than five minutes. I think you're going to survive."

"Can't you just go away?"

"Sorry, no can do. I have a rule against letting beautiful woman turn into blocks of ice on my watch."

She opened her eyes to find him gazing down at her, a skate on each side of her head. "Don't call me beautiful."

"Why not?"

He looked amused. Amused! She was in mortal agony and he was entertained. Beast. "Because it makes me have difficulty suppressing my fantasies about you."

He lifted an eyebrow. "You have fantasies? What kind?"

Oh, hell. Even if he was Mr. Ethics when it came to Alexis, that didn't give Cassie the liberty to start drooling openly. Time to change the topic. "Why do you find it so amusing to see me on the brink of death?"

"What's entertaining is seeing my strong and mighty Cassie reduced to a whimpering female."

She glared at him, trying to look as imposing as she could when stretched out on her back on a frozen pond. "First, I'm not *your* Cassie. And second, I am most definitely not a whimpering female. Both terms are inaccurate and offensive."

"You're lucky I'm in a good mood or I might take offense at your taking offense at my calling you 'my Cassie.' I'm not such a bad guy."

"You get only one woman to call yours, and you already have one. So don't be putting any possessive pronouns before my name. It might discourage other suitors." Besides, that stupid possessive pronoun made her stomach go all wiggly. *Ty's Cassie.* Did that have a nice ring to it or what?

It certainly seemed that allowing herself to fantasize about him really wasn't making her feel any better. What did she expect? Leo was the one who'd given her that advice and what did Leo know? Who was the stress therapist around here, huh? That would be her, not Leo.

Obviously, Cassie needed to go with her gut, which was very clearly instructing her never to think about Ty as a man again. Period. Easy enough. Uh-huh.

"Wouldn't want to discourage your admirers, now would I?" He skated around her until he was standing between her legs. He extended his hands to her. "Come on, I'll help you."

Just as another complaint about the stupidity of the sport occurred to her, she noticed that there was a twinkle in Ty's eyes and a smile curving his lips. Huh. He looked like he was in a good mood. She was certain it was the first time she'd ever seen a real smile on his face, at least one that wasn't accentuated with tense lines around his mouth. A hint of pride settled in her chest. It certainly appeared she was beginning to have at least a modicum of success, didn't it?

Damn, she was good.

But that meant she had to get off her butt—literally—and continue with the therapy.

"Fine." She lifted her hands off the ice and placed her puffy blue mittens into his black leather gloves. "You offered."

Ty grinned and whisked her to her feet, apparently having no trouble keeping his balance while he helped with hers.

"Show-off."

"Hey, I played hockey. It's my one skill."

As if she believed for a minute that Ty was a man of limited skills. "What about pizza? Can't you cook a mean pizza?"

"The meanest." Still holding her hands, he began to skate backward, pulling her gently along. "Just relax. I won't let you fall."

"I'm not worried about falling." Could she feel more uncoordinated? Note to self: ice skates and her body were not a good combination.

"Just about landing, huh? I've heard that one before."

But he was smiling, his wool trench coat flapping

lightly around his denim-clad calves as he moved lithely across the ice. Even her mention of pizza hadn't taken the smile off his face. Was this all it took to lighten the man up? Some ice and some blades? "So...does Alexis skate?"

"Nope."

Hmm. "Maybe you could get her out here?"

"She doesn't do athletic things. More of an indoor kind of gal." Ty pulled Cassie closer, then spun her around so her back was pressed against his front. "Let's switch directions. I want to see where I'm going. Too many crazy kids out here to crash into."

But his voice was warm and he'd been trading friendly jousts with the kids as they breezed by him, brandishing their hockey sticks.

Ty pulled her close and wrapped his arms around her waist, anchoring her to him. Then he began to skate, pushing her forward. "Move your feet in rhythm with mine," he instructed. "Don't worry about your balance. I have you."

"I'm not a skater." *I have you.* How was it possible that those three little words could send chills down her spine and make her belly quiver?

"Just try."

Try? How was she supposed to concentrate on skating with Ty crushing her against him, his thighs brushing against hers with every stroke? She couldn't feel a single bruise anymore and her blood was heating every inch of her body. The healing power of a man's touch.

"Move your feet with mine, Cass."

All righty, then.

She could do this.

Concentrate on his feet, Cassie.

She shook her head to clear it, grabbed Ty's arms tightly just in case he forgot to hold her up, then tried to mimic his leisurely, graceful strides. Right, left, right, left. "Hey, I'm getting it."

"Of course you are." He dropped his head, resting his cheek against hers as they skated together. "Turn coming up. Just lean against me and follow my body."

Yes, she would be having dreams about this moment for the rest of her life. Skating hopelessly erotic? She'd never have thought it.

"Relax, Cassie. Trust me."

"I do." She did trust him, and as more than a skating partner. She knew she could give him her heart and he'd take care of it—hypothetically speaking, of course. If Ty dedicated himself to her, she knew she'd be able to count on him even if he was thrust into a roomful of gorgeous naked women. So what if it was Alexis he'd given himself to? What it meant was that there was at least one man worth trusting in this world. If there was one, there must be others. So maybe, just maybe, there was a chance Cassie wouldn't have to avoid dating for the next eighty years.

She sighed, relaxed against him and felt him nod against her cheek.

"There you go. Skating can be fun."

"I'm beginning to figure that out."

They were quiet for a while, skating in perfect rhythm, their bodies moving as one.

"Zach skates, too," Ty said finally.

"Well, then. Maybe I'll have to get him to go skating with me. I imagine this could be romantic with the right guy." As if she'd ever skate with Zach. How could she taint this perfect memory?

"What about with the wrong guy?" Ty's words were soft, whispered in her ear.

"It can be romantic with the wrong guy, too." Understatement of the year. No, of the decade. No, the millennium.

He grunted and tightened his grip on her.

Forty-five minutes later, Cassie's quads and calves were screaming in protest. Even Ty's warm body against her couldn't give her quivering limbs strength. "Ty, I need to sit for a bit. I'm a little out of shape." Perhaps it would have helped if she'd recently had exercise other than shoveling chocolate into her mouth.

"Sure." He guided her to the edge of the pond and helped her off the ice, through the crusted snow to a fallen tree serving as a makeshift bench. "Thanks. That was great."

She looked up at him then, saw his flushed cheeks, his dancing eyes. The man had been handsome when his face was lined with stress, but now he looked positively heavenly. Rugged and masculine in his jeans, sophisticated in his wool trench coat and black leather gloves. He had everything. Except her.

She giggled to herself. Wasn't that a kick, pretending Ty was the unlucky one because he didn't get her? She rather liked that line of thinking, actually. Might tuck it away for future reference.

Ty stood in front of her, watching the boys practicing hockey at the far end of the pond. Was that a hankering she saw in his eyes? Hmm... "Why don't you keep skating?" she suggested.

"Don't be silly. I'll leave with you." He dropped down beside her on the log and propped one skate over his knee to begin unlacing it.

"No, I'll wait." Cassie put her mitten over his fingers

and pointed to the ice with her other hand. "Go shoot the puck with them for a bit."

"Really?"

"Of course." As if she'd take him away from the one activity she'd found that made him alive again. Relaxed and happy. De-stressed. Watching him skate would give her a chance to bask in the glory of her success. And if she got a little zing from watching him glide, well, then, that wasn't her fault, was it?

"You're the best." He dropped a quick kiss on her forehead, then plowed back through the snow to the pond, shooting across the ice toward the bevy of young boys milling around a portable net.

While her forehead burned from his kiss, Cassie propped her chin on her hands and watched Ty play with the kids. The boys gaped in awe when he showed off, then screamed for him to show them how to do the same.

No doubt, Ty would make a perfect father.

Jealous? Her? Not a chance. She was simply making an objective observation. Nothing wrong with that, was there?

TY DIDN'T STOP until it was too dark to see the black puck on the ice. After high-fiving the kids in farewell, he glided back across the pond.

What an excellent day.

He couldn't recall the last time he'd been on skates, let alone taken an afternoon just to enjoy himself. A quick stop sprayed ice flecks across Cassie's feet and he grinned. "Thanks, Cassie."

"N-n-no problem."

"Cassie?" He vaulted off the ice, his blades sinking into the crusty snow. "What's wrong?"

"N-n-nothing." Her cheeks were pale and she was hugging herself. Her hat was pulled down almost to her eyelashes and she'd zipped her parka up to her nose. She was jogging in place with quick little steps and she was shivering.

"You're freezing." Guilt surged through him. "Why didn't you say anything?"

"You were having fun."

"So what?" He pulled off his overcoat and wrapped it around her. "It's winter out here."

"Hadn't noticed."

"Yeah, right." He grabbed her skates, picked up his boots, slung his arm around her shoulder and hauled her up against him to infuse her with some of his warmth. "Back to the car. You can sit in the heat while I change out of my skates."

"I'm fine...really," she said, belying her words by burrowing against him.

"Martyr." She felt good pressed against him. Too good. But he couldn't push her away, for her own sake. She was cold and she needed him.

"Top-notch stress management consultant, you mean."

"That, too." They reached the car and he pulled open the passenger door. "I have to admit I had an unbelievable time today. Sit."

She sat, her body still shaking visibly.

This wasn't good.

"Hell, Cassie. You're way too cold." He reached around her, put the key in the ignition and started his car. "What about your grandpa whose face was paralyzed for a month because of frostbite?"

"I recall that story only when it's convenient for me to do so. It wasn't convenient."

"You're insane."

"No, I'm good."

"Fine. You're good. And you're insane." He finished untying his laces, yanked the skates off and tossed them in the back seat. He shoved his feet into his boots, shut Cassie's door and ran around to the driver's side. "Warming up yet?"

"Like burnt toast."

"Liar." Ty cranked up the heat, which seemed pitifully inadequate to halt the tremors rattling Cassie's body. "Fifteen minutes and we'll be home."

She nodded and Ty pulled his overcoat more tightly around her, buttoning it under her chin. "Why didn't you wait in the car?"

"Because I was having fun watching you."

He lifted his eyebrows and a warm feeling settled over him. "Really?"

"No, actually I was frozen to the log." She snuggled deeper into his overcoat. "Does this car have seat heat?"

"Yep." He flicked the switch and gunned the engine. "Twelve minutes. We'll be home in twelve."

"I'll be dead by then," she grumbled.

"At least then I'd be spared further therapy."

"But you'd be wrought with guilt for the rest of your life that I froze to death waiting for you. You'll be tortured and demented. It would be an ugly end to such a promising life."

"Then I guess I'd better keep you alive, huh?"

Cassie closed her eyes. "It would definitely be in your best interest."

In more ways than he cared to admit.

BY THE TIME THEY GOT to his house, Cassie hadn't stopped shaking and color hadn't returned to her cheeks. And no matter how many times he scolded her for letting herself get so cold, she didn't appear the least bit repentant.

A woman of strong convictions.

He loved it.

Not her.

It. Her strength.

"Sit." He pointed to the couch. "I'll get you a blanket and start a fire."

"I can just go home...." He grabbed her ankles and upended her on the couch. "Or I can lie down on the couch."

"Much better answer. Stay."

"I'm not a dog."

"Really? Hadn't noticed." Ty sprinted out of the living room and up the stairs, grabbing the comforter off his bed. Back down the stairs, around the corner...and *phew*. She was still there. With Cassie, he wouldn't have been surprised to find her already driving down the street like a crazed lunatic.

"Here." He dumped the comforter on top of her, then tucked it around her. "This should start to warm you up."

She poked her head out from under the blanket. "You don't need to take care of me."

"Humor me. I feel it's my fault you got so cold, because I wasn't paying attention to you."

"Fine." She pulled the comforter back over her head, disappearing from view. "How's this?" Her voice was muffled and he grinned.

"Perfect." Damn, it felt good to be taking care of her. It was about time she let him.

It took only a few minutes to get a roaring fire

started. By the time he returned from the kitchen with two cups of hot chocolate, Cassie had migrated to the carpet in front of the fireplace. She had kicked off her boots and was rubbing her sock feet.

"Feet cold?"

"I'm not sure. It could just be that all the nerves have died and I don't the capacity to feel anymore."

Ty handed her one of the mugs. "Here. I'll take over."

"It's okay…."

"Indulge me."

She shrugged and wrapped her hands around the mug. "Fine."

Ty set his mug on the hearth and pulled Cassie's feet onto his lap. Did she have cute feet or what? Not that he cared. He was simply rubbing her feet to get them warm. "So…um…thanks for today. I had fun."

She opened her eyes slightly, peering at him from beneath her eyelashes. "You sound surprised."

"I am, I guess. I haven't taken an afternoon to play for a long time. Years."

"Think you'll do it again?"

He paused, then nodded. "I don't think I have a choice."

"Meaning?"

"I don't think I'd be able to make myself sit at the computer all the time anymore."

Cassie smiled, looking so warm and so pleased that he felt like hugging her. He massaged her feet instead.

"Are you going to join an ice hockey league?" she asked.

Not a bad idea. "Hadn't thought of that."

"Or coach a kids' ice hockey team?"

He grinned. "I think I'd enjoy that."

"I think you would, too." She wiggled deeper into the blanket and sighed with satisfaction. "I am a true goddess. Only days to spare and you're healed."

"It's not like I'm totally changing," he said. "I'll still have to work a lot."

"Because you need to accumulate more funds to open your pizza place?"

"No. For Alexis. To give her security."

"Don't let go of your dream, Ty."

He wrapped his hands around her foot. "Sometimes dreams have to wait."

"Don't wait too long."

"What's *your* dream, Cassie?" Though the question was designed to direct the focus of the conversation away from him, the moment it was out of his mouth, he knew he wanted to know the answer.

She sighed. "I wanted tons of kids."

"You don't anymore?"

"Well, it takes time to have kids. Now that I have to start over, I'm not sure how much time I'll end up having. One will be fine."

"Cassie! You're twenty-seven years old. You could still have a dozen kids if you wanted them." Kids with another man. That was a pleasant thought. Pleasant as in how it would be pleasant to have a pit bull tear off his hand. "All your kids will be completely stress-free. Or afraid to ride in cars. One or the other."

She wrinkled her nose. "I don't always drive like that."

"You must not or you'd have killed yourself by now."

"Was it really that bad?"

"I had nightmares for a week."

"Well, I'm better now. I apologize for the fiasco with

the car. I'm feeling fine. Over that little episode." She pursed her lips. "You know, I wanted to give up on you, but Leo wouldn't let me. But now that I succeeded with you, I feel much better. I'm not a total failure." Cassie propped herself up on her elbow. "I even did the right thing with Drew, you know? What if I'd been stuck with him?" She shook her head and flopped back down. "Can you even imagine being married to the wrong person? Imagine what a mess I'd be if we'd already been married."

Can you imagine being married to the wrong person? The words burned into Ty's brain as Cassie continued to talk, her words muffled by the screaming in his mind.

Finally, he dropped her foot and stared at her.

She stopped talking. "What's wrong?"

"I'm not in love with Alexis."

12

CASSIE'S EYES WIDENED and her face drained of color. *"What?"*

"I'd never been in love in my life and Alexis was my best friend. She needed me. So I told her I'd marry her." He grimaced. "Love wasn't an issue."

Cassie pulled her foot out his hands. "I really don't think I'm qualified to be counseling you on this."

"Why not?"

She held up her hand. "Trust me. I'm not."

"I don't care about your qualifications." And he didn't. He simply needed to talk. To Cassie. He needed her. How about that, huh? For the first time in his life, he actually needed someone else. He knew he should feel completely uncomfortable with that concept, but he didn't. It felt right to have Cassie be the one he needed.

He stretched out beside her, six inches of fluffy comforter safely between them. "Alexis doesn't love me, either."

Cassie squirmed to her left, away from him. "That's great. Oops! Did you hear my car honk? It's time for me to leave."

Ty clapped a heavy hand on her hip and anchored her to the carpet. "Where are you going?"

"Wherever my car takes me."

"Why are you leaving? You've been trying to get me

to talk about what's really going on with Alexis ever since you and I met. Now that I am, you won't listen?" He felt as if he was on the verge of some monumental revelation, but he couldn't quite open the door by himself. He needed her strength.

"Because I don't want to be responsible for destroying Alexis's life," Cassie snapped.

Ty dropped his hand from her hip, startled by the venom in her voice. "What are you talking about?"

"Oh, come on, Ty." She sat up and pulled the comforter around her. "Are you blind?"

"Apparently so. Blind about what?"

For a moment, hesitation and doubt flickered over her face. "Finish what you were saying."

"I lost the flow."

Cassie sighed and met his gaze…and he was startled by the stark vulnerability in her eyes. "You don't love Alexis. Alexis doesn't love you. It's not my fault. Go on."

"Why would it be your fault? I've known Alexis for twenty years and we've never been in love." He tried to touch Cassie's cheek, but she ducked out of his reach.

"Why are you telling me this?"

Ty sighed and lay on his back, staring at the ceiling. "For the last two years, it's never bothered me a bit, knowing I would marry Alexis even though we weren't in love. We even talked about it when I proposed, and we both agreed it didn't matter. We were best friends. She was with me the day I cried because I got in trouble at school when I was six. I was the one she told about her first kiss. We had no secrets from each other."

"Sounds like a great relationship," Cassie said, her voice flat.

"It is. Or it was." He had such a headache. "But lately..." *Just say it.* "I've wondered whether it was the right thing. For both of us. Doesn't she deserve love?" But it was about more than love, too. "She also deserves the security I can give her."

"I sense a 'but'...."

"So do I."

"What is it?"

He shook his head. "I don't know."

Cassie groaned and flopped back on the floor, stretching out beside him. He could hear her breathing, and wondered if she was looking at the same spot on the ceiling he was.

Probably. They had that kind of connection.

"I think I know what it is," she said quietly.

"You do?" She smelled so good, so close. He could just roll over and she'd be right there....

"It's my fault," she said.

"How?"

"I—I—" She drew a loud breath. "I've sort of fallen for you. And I'm sure you can tell and that's why you're confused, because I've been sending you signals, but I didn't mean to and I'm sorry and that's why I didn't want to help you originally, and plus—"

Ty sat up, his heart racing. "What do you mean, you've fallen for me?" He didn't want to hear her answer, but at the same time, he had to know.

"I've fallen in love with you." She immediately jumped to her feet and sprinted to the other side of the room behind an oversize moving box. "I'm so sorry. I never would have said anything, but I know that's what happened. I swear I'm not a home-wrecker. I just wanted to make you have fun and follow your dream because I thought that's what was stressing you. If I'd realized this whole thing about Alexis... I would have stayed away. I didn't realize you were vulnerable...."

"You love me?"

"Umm...sort of."

"Like a friend?"

"That, too."

"Like a..." He couldn't say the words. His mind was spinning so fast he couldn't even send the signals to his mouth to speak.

"In love, Ty. I'm *in love* with you."

The words hung in the air, danced through the flames, flirted with the smoke from the fire, then settled in his gut. "I didn't know."

"And you shouldn't. But you're officially de-stressed and we don't need to be together anymore."

"I... You..."

"Don't say it."

"You're special, Cass. I've known it since the first day we met."

She covered her ears. "Shut up, Ty."

"Why?"

"Don't you see?" She picked up a smaller box and put it on top of the one she was standing behind. A bigger fortress. "You restored my faith in men. Because you're loyal to your fiancée. You aren't even in love with her and yet you'll honor your vows? You're a hero, Ty. A hero."

"Not even close." He stood up and walked toward Cassie.

"Stay away from me, Ty."

"You love me." He still couldn't believe it. It made him feel like the luckiest man in the world. He was certain he could leap to the moon right now if he tried. "You actually love me."

"Ah, yeah. That's the stickler." She added another box to the barricade. "See, I love you because you're worth loving. I know I can trust you."

He walked around the left side of Cassie's roadblock and she moved the other way, keeping the boxes between them.

"But, you see, Ty, if you abandon your vows to Alexis for me, then you become like any other man."

Ty stopped and frowned. "What do you mean?"

"You become like Drew. Walking away from commitment when you find something better. I'd always be afraid you'd find someone else."

"I'd never leave you, Cassie. I'd swear on my life."

"But you're marrying Alexis."

A lump of coal settled in his gut. "I have to. For her."

"See? That's why I love you. Because you'll be there for Alexis to the end."

"So, even if I decided not to marry Alexis..."

Cassie shook her head. "Then you'd be leaving her. For someone else. And then...how do I know you wouldn't do it to me?"

"I wouldn't."

"Besides, then I'd always feel guilty for interfering. I didn't mean to fall in love with you, I swear." She picked up a sizeable box and held it against her chest. "After what I went through with Drew, no way could I ever be a part of doing that to someone else."

She began to back toward the couch, keeping the box between them.

Ty couldn't stop the corners of mouth from curving up. "Are you stealing my box?"

She glanced down in surprise. "Oh." She set it on the

table, then shoved her feet into her boots. "Sorry. Instinct."

"You have an instinct to steal?"

"No. To protect myself from you." She picked up her coat and shrugged it on.

"What am I going to do to you?"

"Anything! All you have to do is look at me the wrong way and I love you more."

"Really?" He grinned, then frowned. "I mean, I don't try to do that."

Cassie rolled her eyes and pulled her stocking cap over her head. "Well, duh. That's what makes you so attractive. I'd hardly be dreaming about you every night if you were some egoistic male *trying* to make women fall in love with him."

Not women.

Just you.

Whoa. Ty frowned. Had he been trying to make Cassie fall in love with him? Of course not. "I set you up with my brother."

"I'm aware of that." Cassie pulled her mittens on. "And you know, I'm not sure that's going to work. I mean, if we had to spend holidays together and stuff…it'd be a little awkward."

Damned if he didn't feel relieved she wasn't interested in Zach. "Holidays would be fine, Cassie." Now why was he doing that? To try to prove that he wasn't thrilled she loved him?

"No, they wouldn't. I'm afraid I might be, um, hostile toward Alexis."

He grinned. "I might be a little hostile toward Zach."

Cassie screeched and covered her ears. "Don't say that!"

"Why not? Why is it okay for you to tell me you love

me, but not okay for me to admit I might be a little jealous of Zach?"

"Because you're the one who's engaged!"

Ah, excellent point. "You're right."

"And don't you forget it." She pulled her car keys out of her pocket. "Now, you have to clean this house for your bride. Do it, don't complain, and get a dog."

"A dog?"

"Yes. A dog will make you get outside every day and have a little fun." Ty took a step toward her and she bolted for the door.

He knew she was never coming back.

Loneliness surged over him and he sprinted after her, catching her as she reached the entranceway. "Stay."

She lifted her chin. "Are you going to leave Alexis?"

Silence hung forever in the hallway. He thought of Cassie, their kiss at the New Year's Eve party, how it had rattled him to his bones.

And then he thought of Alexis.

Alone.

Scared.

Depending on him.

He cursed and closed his eyes.

"That's why I love you," Cassie said softly. "You'll always be my hero, Ty. Always."

She touched his face and he opened his eyes to find her gazing at him, with so much love he nearly knelt in humble gratitude.

Then she slipped her hand behind his neck and tugged gently.

He bent and she touched her lips to his, so softly, like a butterfly bumping against his lips. Beautiful, evasive and gone before he could respond.

"Bye, Ty."

He couldn't bring himself to answer, watching her slip out his front door and shut it quietly behind her.

And for the first time in his adult life, he felt the burn of tears in his eyes.

He shook his head immediately. Enough of that. He was buying himself a dog. A pit bull. The dog of a man who didn't fall in love. Men who owned pit bulls didn't cry.

Or maybe half pit bull and half wolf.

And he'd name the dog Killer.

Ty looked at his watch. Four-thirty. The shelter probably closed at five.

Watch out, Killer.

I'm coming to get you.

"So, seen Ty lately?" Cassie asked as she tied the bow on the assorted treats gift bag at Leo's store. Cassie had been there an hour and hadn't eaten even one piece of chocolate. What was the point? It wasn't going to help.

It had been exactly seven days and five hours since she'd walked out of Ty's house, and she hadn't been able to stop thinking about him. She'd gone into seclusion for five full days, but then her hair had gotten so itchy from not showering, and she really wasn't feeling any better, so she'd given up.

And now she was stuck in the world of the living and functioning, wishing she had anyone's life but her own.

Sometimes.

At other times, she was quite certain she would recover nicely and have a wonderful, fulfilling life. Okay, fine, that had been once for five seconds when she'd thought she'd seen Drew's name in the obituaries, but still, that was progress.

"Actually, yes. Ty stopped by the store yesterday to buy some items," Leo said.

"Really? What did he say?" She wanted to know how he was doing. That was perfectly normal. He was her client, after all. Of course she'd want to check on his progress. It didn't mean she hadn't picked up her life and moved on.

Leo pulled a tray of fudge out of the cooler. "He said he'd totally unpacked his whole house for Alexis. Looks like you did good with him."

"Great." Whoops. She sounded disappointed. "That's great!" A truly ebullient response. She should be on Broadway.

Leo lifted an eyebrow.

Or maybe Cassie wasn't such a great actress, after all.

"So, did he say when Alexis was due in town?" Why was she doing this to herself? Why couldn't she pretend he didn't exist?

"He was buying the chocolates for her, actually. She comes in tonight." Leo's voice was filled with quiet sympathy.

Cassie's throat closed up and she immediately started coughing.

Leo was beside her in an instant. "I'm so sorry, hon. I wasn't going to tell you, but then I thought it was better to hear it from me. Do you need to cry? We could go in the back and..."

Cassie lifted her head and looked at Leo, who was wearing sparkly blue eye shadow. Blue. It seemed so strange for someone to be wearing such a cheery color.

Shouldn't everyone be wearing black or something? "I'm fine."

"Really?" Leo didn't look convinced. "You know, it's good she's finally coming back. It'll force you to get over him."

"I know," Cassie sighed. Heaven help her, she was so tired of feeling this way.

"And think of it like this. At least you know there are men out there worth trusting. That must help, huh? You didn't believe that for a long time."

"I suppose."

"Obviously you can't be that worried about being with a guy if you let yourself fall in love with Ty. If you were incapable of ever trusting again, it wouldn't have happened."

It made sense in a perverse sort of way.

"Plus you helped Ty with his stress, so you obviously still have your career."

"That's true." She had proved that, hadn't she?

"So, the only thing left is to get over him."

Oh, right. No problem at all.

Leo leaned against the counter. "I have a date tonight with a stockbroker. Why don't I call him and have him bring a friend? Then you won't sit at home thinking about the reunion at Ty's house."

"Thanks for the visual." Cassie slapped the side of her head before she could start envisioning Alexis in Ty's arms.

"So, are you going to come? Was your five-day pity-fest enough to make you realize that pining solves nothing?"

Cassie lifted her chin. What else was she going to do? Give up the rest of her life for a man who was married to someone else? As fun as that sounded, she wanted more than that. "I'll go."

"You will?"

"Sure." It was time. She was ready to get back in the ring. This time she'd bring a gun and wear brass knuckles just in case she came across a lecherous cretin. But she was also ready to accept that there were decent men out there.

Well, there was one, at least.

And he was taken.

She scowled.

Why *did* she keep doing that to herself? There was simply no sense in even remembering that Ty existed.

While Leo dialed her cellphone and ordered another man for the evening, Cassie closed her eyes and rubbed her temples.

You will not think about Ty tonight. You will not think about Ty tonight. You will not think about Ty tonight.

"All set. You, my friend, have a date." Leo swung her arm over Cassie's shoulder. "Let's shut this store down so we can make sure you are scorching hot for your first date in four years."

A date.

She didn't want a date.

She wanted to be with Ty.

Cassie lifted her chin. She couldn't be with Ty. *Get over him and move on.* She'd recovered from Drew and she'd known him for four years. Technically, since she'd known Ty for only a few months, she should be over him in no time.

So why wasn't it working that way?

"YOU GOT A COCKER SPANIEL?" They were the very first words out of Alexis's mouth when Ty picked her up at the airport. Ty and Gracie, his new, satiny black cocker spaniel.

"They were out of wolf–pit bull mixed breeds," he muttered. "And her time was up. I couldn't exactly leave her at the shelter, could I?"

"I never would have pictured you with a cocker spaniel." Alexis pushed the wagging black body out of her face and sat down in the passenger seat. "Okay, let's go."

"All you have is that backpack? What about your other bags?"

She folded her hands in her lap. "I have to go back tomorrow."

Relief surged through him and he was immediately ashamed of himself. "Why didn't you wait until you were all finished?" A car honked at Ty and he pulled away from the curb. "So you could stay?"

"It's nice to see you, Ty."

He gritted his teeth and nodded. "Glad to have you here, Alexis."

She pursed her lips and said nothing.

Silence fell over the car...except for the thumping of Gracie's little tail as she snuggled on Ty's lap.

"Isn't that dangerous? To have the dog on your lap while you're driving?"

"She's still scared. She needs the comfort," Ty said, putting his hand protectively over her head. "And she stays very still. She's a good dog. You'll like her." And of course, Alexis's comment about driving made him think of Cassie and her Formula One driving habits. Why couldn't he stop thinking about her? With Alexis in his car, he couldn't get Cassie out of his mind?

He was despicable.

Alexis sighed and leaned her head back against the

seat. "She's your dog. You're the one who needs to like her."

"And you." He swallowed. "She'll be your dog, too."

Alexis said nothing and he wondered if he'd made a mistake in getting Gracie. He rubbed the soft fur and realized it didn't matter. Gracie was part of his family now and he couldn't give her back. "So, you want to stop at a park and run Gracie around?"

"It's seven o'clock, Ty. And freezing."

"Right."

Silence fell in the car again.

It had never been hard to make conversation with Cassie. Then again, it had never been difficult to talk to Alexis before, either. What was wrong with him? "So, how are you? Good?" Alexis glanced at him and he realized how tired she looked. "Alexis? What's wrong?"

She smiled faintly. "You can still read my mind. Same as when we were kids."

"We've been best friends for a long time," Ty said quietly.

"That we have." She twisted her hands in her lap. "Have you eaten dinner?"

"No. I was going to make us some pizza. I have a new recipe I wanted to try out." It was just a hint, to see what she thought. Not that he'd ever pressure her, but if she suggested it…

"I'm not in the mood for pizza. Can we stop at a restaurant?"

A black cloud settled over Ty's shoulders. "Fine."

IF SHE TRIED REALLY HARD, maybe she could disintegrate him with her brain waves. Cassie narrowed her eyes and focused on the blabbering idiot across the table from her.

Nothing.

Her psychic attack didn't even slow him down, let alone dissolve him into nothingness.

Sure, he appeared to be smart. And his suit looked expensive. And his blond hair looked sort of thick. And he'd brought her flowers.

But he was dull.

And she was bored.

Perhaps she could claim cramps? Or strep throat? Or maybe the highly contagious whooping cough?

"So, everyone up for a movie after dinner?" Leo nudged Cassie with her knee, looking decidedly cheerful. Then again, Leo tended to withhold judgment on her escorts until the date had been fully consummated. It took a serious hygiene problem or a dangerous prison record for Leo to bail early. And even then...

"I'm a little tired," Cassie said, giving a weak hack that would never pass muster as whooping cough.

"Tired? It's not even eight o'clock."

"I'm...*tired*." She coughed again, trying to make it rattle in her chest. No luck.

Leo cocked a knowing eyebrow. "Are you now?"

"Yes."

"I think not." She lowered her voice and leaned toward Cassie. "No one said your first date was going to be easy. Give the guy a chance."

"I'm trying," Cassie whispered. "He's just not my type."

"There's only one Ty. Get another type," Leo hissed, flashing a sparkling smile at the men across the table, no doubt to blind them for a moment so she could finish lecturing Cassie.

"Ty isn't the only one I could ever like." She just wasn't particularly attracted to this man. He wasn't as funny as Ty or as warm, and he didn't make her blood sing the way Ty did. But that didn't mean she was comparing him to Ty.... Okay, so maybe she needed to work a little harder on forgetting Ty existed. "Fine, I'll stay at least for dessert."

"And a movie."

"Maybe." Only if she couldn't talk her way out of it.

At least her fear of dating had been replaced by a fear of being miserably bored on meaningless dates with rich, handsome stockbrokers.

She was making progress.

THE WOMAN ACROSS the table from him would soon be his wife.

His wife.

Alexis.

The mother of his children.

She lifted her linen napkin off the table and unfolded it across her lap. Her cheeks were pale, and Ty noted dark smudges under her eyes. He frowned. "Are you all right?"

"We need to talk."

"About the wedding? Whatever you want to do is fine with me." Their wedding. What a thought. He couldn't do it. No, he could. It would just take a little while to get used to Alexis again.

"Do you love me, Ty?"

"Of course."

She folded her hands around the stem of her wine-glass. "I meant, are you in love with me?"

Ty gritted his teeth. "We've talked about this be-fore."

"I wanted to see if your feelings had changed. But they haven't, have they? You're not in love with me?"

"It doesn't matter, Alexis. I'll be here for you forever."

Alexis looked at him. "That's the thing, Ty. It does matter. I want to marry a man who's in love with me."

He swallowed. "Maybe we'll get to that point. We haven't been around each other—"

"I'll never be in love with you."

He blinked. "What?"

Alexis reached across the table and laid her hand on his. Her fingers were like ice. "I love you, Ty. But I don't want to marry you. I don't need to marry you."

Ty shook his head. "What did you say?"

Her cheeks turned pink. "I don't want you to take care of me."

"What?"

"You're like my big brother, always telling me what to do and trying to keep me cocooned in a safe little place." She shifted in her chair. "I needed you two years ago, but I'm different now."

"You're dumping me?" His mind was spinning, the earth rattling under his feet.

"It's not like that. It's just... Well..." She took a drink of wine. "When I thought about being married fifty years from now, I knew we'd never make it. Being best friends isn't enough for a marriage, Ty. There has to be more."

He leaned back in his seat and let his breath out. "I can't believe this."

She tried to smile, but her eyes were brimming with tears. "I didn't want to hurt you. But...I didn't know what else to do. I've been avoiding coming back because I didn't know what to do or..."

"No, no, no. Don't cry." He leaned forward and took her hands. "Are you sure about this? Was it something I did?" If he drove her away, he'd never forgive himself.

"No!" She shook her head. "I've been trying to hint at it for months, but you always ignored it. Just kept telling me how you'd protect me and everything." A small smile curved her lips. "You can be really difficult sometimes."

He almost smiled. "I've been hearing that a lot lately."

"So, you're not mad?"

He smiled then. "I love you, Alexis, but I really didn't want to have to see you naked."

A disbelieving laugh fell from her lips. "Really?"

"I swear."

"I didn't want to see you naked, either," she said.

"I look good in the buff."

She smiled, laughter making her eyes dance. "I'm sure you do. But...it sort of gave me nightmares, thinking about it."

"I'm offended."

"No, you're not. You're relieved because you didn't really want to parade around without clothing in front of me, anyway."

Ty laughed and squeezed her hand. "As usual, you know me too well."

Alexis let out a big sigh. "Whew. I feel so much better now. I was worried."

"About having to see me in my birthday suit?"

She grinned. "About this whole visit. Nudity included. That's actually why I didn't want to eat at your house tonight. I was afraid you'd set up some seduction scene and it would be really awkward, with you standing there naked while I was telling you..."

"That I'm too much like your brother to marry?"

"Yes. But I still love you and I want to be able to call you and complain about everything yucky in my life for the next fifty years."

"You got it." He was free. Alexis had granted him his freedom. Unbelievable. His heart felt like it was defying gravity; his shoulders felt like they were dancing.

"So, how about I sleep in your guest room tonight?" Alexis said. "And tell me about this new pizza recipe. When are you going to open your pizza store? You must have enough money saved up by now."

He grinned. "Very soon, Alexis. Very soon."

13

"SHALL I COME IN for a drink?" Cassie's date asked with a cocky leer.

She wondered if it would be rude to pick up a pile of snow and smash it in his persistent face. "No, thanks."

"You sure?" He lifted his hands toward her waist to suck her in for a good-night kiss. Hadn't he noticed the lack of chemistry during the movie, when she'd set the popcorn and soda between them so he couldn't fondle her knee or tickle her elbow?

"Oh, did you hear that? I think a cockroach is drowning in my toilet. I must run." She ducked inside, nearly taking off his fingers when he stuck his hand in the door to stop her.

Darn. So close to victory. It would have been a fitting end to the evening to smash those roving fingers in her door.

Wait a sec. What was that smell? Oregano? Bread? Garlic? In her house?

She pressed her back against the front door. "Leo?" Wait. It couldn't be Leo; they'd just double-dated.

Silence.

"Evil murderous rapist?"

Silence.

Cassie's heart started racing and her breath became tight in her throat. Okay, no need to panic. Since when would a burglar cook? Or order in Italian food?

Date From Hell knocked on the door and said something about using her phone.

Great.

Stalker outside.

Intruder inside.

Was she lucky or what?

Cassie inched her way to her right and tripped over the ice skates she'd dropped on the floor after her skating evening with Ty. Skates she'd tossed aside in an aggravated heap and refused to acknowledge ever since.

Perfect.

She picked up the skates and slid a hand in each one, all the way to the toes.

Blades up. *Just try and fight me.* "I'm armed."

No response.

Date From Hell knocked on the door again, rambling about dead car batteries. As if she'd believe that ploy. The man had an eighty-thousand-dollar car with about six thousand miles on it. Did he really think she was that stupid?

"I'm coming," she said.

Her date muttered something appreciative. Yeah, right. As if she was coming to rescue *him*.

The intruder had probably been casing her house while she was lying on the floor in her sweats surrounded by tissues. Big mistake. Just because she'd been a sniveling, pathetic loser for the last week didn't mean she was a pushover who wouldn't defend her home. He had no idea how tough she was. Now that she'd survived her first real date in four years, nothing could stop her.

"I'm a black belt and I'm in a really bad mood," she said, keeping her voice deep and scary. She had plenty of built up hostility against men. Sure, she was recovered, but she'd never had the opportunity to truly vent. A testosterone-laden assailant was precisely what she needed to cleanse her system of all lingering animosity.

She almost hoped he'd still be there when she reached the kitchen. It would be fun to do some pummeling. She lifted the skates higher, their metal blades deadly weapons in her hands. "I'm almost to the kitchen," she warned. "You better get away while you still can."

She shuffled along the hall, the hairs on her arms rigid. She contemplated growling and baring her teeth. That'd scare him, no doubt thinking he'd stumbled into the house of a total crazy woman.

A month ago, he would have been right.

Now, she was just a tough chick no longer willing to roll over for the opposite sex.

The light in the kitchen was on.

A pot clanked. Her heart thudded. Okay, so maybe she didn't *really* want to engage in hand-to-hand combat with a deranged killer. "Leo? Are you sure it isn't you? You better let me know so I don't kill you by accident." Even though it couldn't possibly be Leo, she could still hope.

Cassie heard a chuckle. A chuckle? How dare someone not take her seriously?

She took a deep breath, lifted the skates higher, then leaped into the doorway, feet apart, legs braced, blades flashing. Ready for battle.

"Hi, Cassie." Ty was lounging against the counter, his hands resting loosely on his hips, a dash of flour on his cheek. "Hungry?"

"Ty?" What? She was so confused.

"I made a new recipe and I wanted your opinion on it. It's almost ready."

"You...we...what...?" He was here. In her kitchen. "Alexis..." She dropped her hands and the skates slid off.

"Cassie! Watch out!"

Too late. The blades descended. Pain shot up her legs; tears sprung to her eyes. "I'm okay," she managed to whimper, hobbling over to the table. "I'm fine. Only a tickle."

Ty was on the ground in front of her before she was even settled, peeling off the three-inch spike heels she'd borrowed from Leo. "Next time you drop a blade on your foot, wear your boots, or at least invest in some skate guards."

"I'll keep that in mind," she muttered. He looked so good. Though his eyebrows were knitted in concern about the possible amputation of her toes, his eyes were light and happy.

Great. So Alexis made him happy. Cassie was so thrilled by that bit of news.

"Just a little cut. You should be okay. Do you have any bandages around here?" Ty hopped to his feet and began opening cabinets. "Any antibiotic cream?"

"How did you get in here?"

"One of the panes on your back door needs to be replaced."

"You broke in?"

"That sounds a bit judgmental," he said. "I prefer to think of it as creatively solving the problem of an obstinate door. Especially since I cleaned up the glass. Ah, success." He grabbed the first aid items and returned to Cassie's feet. "I didn't know where your spare key was."

"I don't have one."

"We'll have to take care of that, then. Or you can just

give me my own." He lifted her foot and propped it on his thigh.

"Your own key? Why would I give you a key to my house?"

"So I can come in when you're not here. Obviously." He spread some cream on her foot and rubbed it softly, just as a movement at the door caught her eye. *A dog?*

"Um, Ty?"

"Yes, darling?"

Darling? Had she not noticed getting a head injury or something? Things were not making sense. "There's a cocker spaniel in my doorway."

"Yes, that's Gracie. You scared her when you came in. She's a little skittish around strangers." He opened a bandage and placed it on her foot. "She's a real sweetie."

"She's yours?"

"You told me to get a dog, so I did. Don't I always do what you tell me to do?" Ty lifted her other foot and placed it against his chest. "This one's a little deeper, but I don't think you'll need stitches."

"You always do what I tell you?"

"Sure."

"I told you to leave me alone and you're not."

"Ah, yes. I have a good reason, though."

"What reason?" The blasted man's eyes were still dancing with delight. Great. She was *so* overjoyed he'd found bliss with the little missus.

"I didn't like that idea," he said, sounding way too chipper.

"Who cares if you didn't like it!" Cassie might be on her way to being recovered and stable, but that didn't mean she was above getting her frying pan out and clocking him with it, to get that love-stricken look off his face. She could cope with only so much, and her threshold was apparently still dangerously low when it came to Ty. "Get away from me."

She tried to tug her foot free, but Ty promptly clamped his hand around her ankle and glowered at her. "Do I look like I'm finished with your foot?"

"Do I look like I care?" She pulled again and he tightened his grip. It felt like an iron vise around her ankle. "I give up. Tell me what you're doing in my house."

"I already told you. I want you to try my new pizza recipe."

"Why don't you have Alexis try it?" Darn it. Way too much venom in that little suggestion. Cassie tried to soften it with a smile. "I mean, she's the one who—"

"She's asleep."

"Oh." That was a little nugget she could have done without. Had Ty exhausted her with his passionate lovemaking?

Not that she cared. At all. Not her. Not a bit.

He spread the cream over her foot, humming softly to himself.

"Why are you in such a good mood?"

"Because I'm in love."

Nice work on asking that question. Ingenious.

Actually, it was good. It was a test of her toughness. Was she really strong enough to survive on her own? You bet. And she'd prove it by asking more questions and not vomiting all over him at his answers. "You're in love?" she asked.

"Yep."

Okay, never mind. She wasn't entirely over him and she didn't want to know.

"Seeing Alexis again changed your feelings?" Why

had she asked that question? As if she wanted to hear the answer. Could she be a bigger idiot? Dumb, dumb, dumb.

"Nope."

"Nope? I don't understand."

Ty finished attaching the second bandage and rested his arms across her thighs, peering up at her. "Would it make you nauseous to see me naked?"

Her mouth dropped open and her mind went blank. Utterly and completely vacant.

For about one second, at which point it promptly filled with the image of Ty without any clothes on. Glorious, wonderful, a fantasy come true.

"Cassie. Answer my question."

"No."

"No, you won't answer my question, or no, it wouldn't make you nauseous to see me in nature's glory?"

"Either. Both."

He grinned. "Good. I'd like to see you naked, too."

She wondered if he'd catch her if she passed out from shock right there.

"So, I guess it's settled then." He stood up and walked to the oven to check the pizza.

"Um...what's settled?"

"That was my test." He grabbed a pot holder and pulled the pizza out, taking a long moment to inhale the tantalizing scent of garlic and oregano. "Mmm. Not as good as a brick oven, but it'll definitely do until I get my ovens installed."

"Ovens?"

"Yes. You'll help me, won't you?"

"Help you what?" The man was completely insane. Or she was the one losing her already tenuous grip on reality, because she couldn't begin to follow his disconnected ramblings.

"Get everything ready. I'll need help to get it open in time for the summer."

Cassie slapped her hands over her ears and shook her head. "Stop it! You're making me crazy!"

Ty grinned, still looking so happy she wanted to push him into a snowdrift. "What's wrong?"

"What test? What ovens? Why are we taking about being naked?"

"Oh, didn't I explain?" Ty picked up a pizza cutter and began slicing his creation. "Alexis told me she couldn't marry me because the thought of seeing me in the buff gave her nightmares, to which I concurred, of course. We're too much like brother and sister to make a go of a romantic relationship. And if we were to get married and have kids, well, the nudity issue would be bound to arise."

"Alexis... You..." Surely she'd finally lost her mind and was imagining this entire scenario.

"Plus, she thinks I'm too controlling. Can you imagine?"

"You are controlling." Stupid thing to say, but what else was she supposed to do? This all had to be a mistake. A delusion. "You're a pain in the butt."

"I know. You control me right back, so we're even. A perfect match, I'd say."

"Us? A perfect match?" Surely she was hallucinating.

Ty raised an eyebrow. "So, anyway, I got a little worried that I wouldn't be a hero in your eyes if I wasn't marrying Alexis. But then I thought it might be okay, since she's the one who dumped me." He tilted his head, the slightest hint of vulnerability in his eyes. "Was I wrong?"

"No." On the off chance this was really happening, she decided to answer.

"So...you could still love me?"

This certainly seemed to be real. Would she be smelling the pizza if she was delirious?

"Cassie?"

"Yes. I could still love you."

He grinned, the deepest smile she'd ever seen. One that penetrated her core. Okay, this had to be real, didn't it? She wouldn't feel as if she was about to explode with love and happiness if she was off in some fantasy, would she?

"When you told me you'd be okay with seeing me naked, I figured that meant you still loved me. You can see now why that was my test, can't you?"

"I guess..." Phew. She was getting hot. Dizzy.

"So, this is the deal. I'm going to go lease that property tomorrow. Cash out my business and open my store by summer. I thought maybe you'd help?" He slipped a piece of pizza onto the plate and set it on the table beside her. "What do you think?"

Think? How could she think right now?

Ty squatted in front of her, framed her face with his hands. "You look pale, Cassie. Are you all right?"

"I feel a little woozy."

"It's my fault, isn't it?"

She nodded.

Ty kissed the tip of her nose. "I'm sorry. I've never been in love before and I'm not really sure how to handle it. Did I make a mess of it?"

"You love me?"

"Well, yes, but that's not the point."

"What's the point?"

"The point is that I'm *in love* with you. There's a difference."

She nodded. "The naked thing."

"Exactly."

"Wow."

"So, I was thinking of going shopping for a ring. Alexis and I never got one, and I kinda want to do it right this time."

"This time?"

Ty took her hands. "This time I'm marrying the woman I dream about. The woman I'm desperately in love with. The woman I want to spend the rest of my life with, have kids with, bake pizza and go ice-skating with."

"You are?"

He cocked a repentant eyebrow. "Oh, wait. Did I forget to ask you?"

"I'm quite sure I'd remember you asking me that kind of thing."

"Darn it. So sorry." He dropped to one knee. "Cassie Halloway, will you marry me?"

This was it. The moment her heart became whole and full and complete. The instant when everything about her life ceased to matter except for the man in front of her.

"Cass?"

"Of course I'll marry you." She was absolutely amazed she'd managed to get those words out in a coherent fashion when her soul was off floating somewhere above her head. No, not floating. Dancing and singing. In perfect rhythm with Ty's soul. She was going to start crying like a blubbering female. So much for being tough. She loved him. Somehow, that didn't feel like such a bad thing right about now. In fact, she was quite certain it was the very best thing that had ever happened to anyone.

He grinned. "Really? You'll marry me?"

"Truly." Through her tears, she smiled back...as if anything in the world could have stopped her from smiling. "How could I turn down a marriage proposal from a man who cooks?"

"That's the only reason you'll marry me?"

"That and the naked thing."

He grinned. "What about love?"

Cassie slid off the chair into his lap and wrapped her arms around his neck. "Love?"

"Yes, love." He pulled her against him, anchored her to his hard body.

Cassie lifted her face to his. "Did I forget to mention how completely, totally and hopelessly in love with you I am?"

"I'm quite sure I'd remember you saying that."

"Well, then. In addition to the fact I can't wait to see you undressed, I'll also marry you because I am completely, totally and hopelessly in love with you and always will be."

"Then I hereby declare us a perfect pair." And he cupped her face and dropped his lips to hers.

Their first real kiss.

First of many.

Epilogue

"Ty! I'm stuck!"

Cassie had barely uttered her plea for help when Ty bounded around the corner, his jeans covered in flour and his boots puffing white clouds with each step. "Had a little accident with the flour," he explained.

"Really? I never would have guessed." Cassie shifted, her feet stuck up in the air, her bottom wedged in the cardboard box of paper cups that had failed in its role as a makeshift chair. Could she be any more undignified? Not that it mattered. She could go bald, turn purple and have her nose swell up to the size of a cantaloupe and Ty would still love her. Gotta love a guy would could love a woman like that. "I could use a little help, Ty."

"I can see that." He bent over her, wrapped his arms around her upper body and hauled her to her feet, steadying her as she wobbled precariously. "Have I told you lately how sexy you are?"

"Last night, actually," Cassie said as she tried to wrap her arms around his neck. "I can't even reach you anymore."

"Don't be ridiculous. No way am I going to let a bellyful of twins keep me from giving you some loving." He plopped down in the box she'd just abandoned, pulling her down on top of him, positioning her sideways across his lap so her enormous belly wasn't in the way. "Zach is cleaning up the flour, so I have a little time. Wanna make out?"

Cassie grinned. "What if someone catches us?" Imagine. They'd been married a year already and her husband still wanted to make out with her. How great was that?

"They'll think we're madly in love and can't keep our hands off each other." He brushed her hair out of her face and kissed her, deeply, thoroughly and with enough passion that all her insides curled with warmth.

"I love you, Ty," she whispered against his lips. "So much."

"You're just saying that because you're hungry and you want me to find you some food," he said. "But I love you, too." Then he patted her belly and bent close to it. "And I love you two troublemakers, as well."

"How do you know they're troublemakers?"

"Twin boys? How could they be anything else but troublemakers?" He shuddered and slipped his hand under her shirt to rest on her belly. "I think of what Zach and I were like as kids.... Yikes. We're going to have to go for some girls after this to balance them."

Cassie grinned and leaned against his chest, her favorite place to be. She snuggled against him. "I was no picnic, either, I hate to tell you. We're in for a challenge either way."

"I love challenges."

Zach popped his head around the corner. "Oh, come on. This is a public place. Would you quit with the mushy stuff?"

"We're just trying to get a little privacy," Ty said. "Too crazy out front."

"Of course it's crazy. It's Friday night. Your restaurant is always packed on Friday nights. Come to the nursery. My gift for you guys arrived. I just finished installing it."

"Really?" *The nursery.* That little phrase had the most amazing sound to it. "Let's go." Cassie tried to stand up, to no avail. "Ty?"

"Right-o, my love." He lifted her effortlessly to her feet, then buried his face in her hair. "I'm not done molesting you, darling, so be prepared when we get home tonight."

"Insatiable." And she loved it. Her husband had turned her into a sexual dynamo. How lucky was she? It was perfect.

He grinned and nipped her earlobe. "What can I say? You're a goddess."

Zach groaned and ushered them down the hallway, muttering something about the restaurant being a family place. Zach pulled open the door to the nursery. "What do you think?"

Cassie waddled through the double-wide door and stopped in stunned astonishment. A huge flat-screen television hung on the wall, atop the pale blue wallpaper. The changing table had been moved aside, replaced by an entertainment center, and speakers hung from the corners of the room. "Holy cow, Zach. This must have cost a fortune."

"What do you think?" He shifted eagerly, like a little kid. "So, do you like it?"

"Um...it goes well with the quilted rocking chair and double cribs."

Zach snorted. "Oh, come on. You guys are going to be stuck back here all the time taking care of those little guys. I figured you'd want some entertainment."

Ty finally laughed. "I'm sure the babies will love

watching *Sesame Street* on surround sound." He grabbed his brother and hugged him. "And so will I. Thanks, man."

Cassie was just getting all misty from the show of brotherly love when Leo walked in. "Where the hell have you been, Zach? I've got a huge line of customers out there, no pizzas to give them and a bunch of screaming kids in the corner."

Zach grimaced. "I was giving Ty and Cassie their present. I've been setting it up for the last couple of hours."

"You had to do it now? I've been at work all day at my store. I'm exhausted, but I come over here because my friend needs my help and because I'm told that you're going to be taking half the load. But where are you? Hanging out watching television!" Leo glared at Ty. "Can't you get a more useful brother?"

Ty grinned. "He's all I've got."

"I can see why Cassie chose you over him." Leo glared at Zach. "And if you flirt with one more female customer, I'm going to cut out your tongue. Have you no concept of being professional?"

Zach gave Cassie a quick hug and a kiss on the cheek. "I'm a wanted man. I must run. Take care." He ducked out of the room, his eyes twinkling. He ruffled Leo's hair as he ran past toward the front of the shop.

Leo shook her head. "Look at me. I'm turning into an ogre. That man drives me crazy."

Cassie hugged her friend. "Thanks for helping out."

"For you, I'll do anything. But it's a good thing I love you or I'd put his head through the veggie chopper." Leo sighed. "I don't know how you put up with men, Cassie. Single life is the only way to go."

Cassie grinned at Ty, who slung his arm around her shoulders. "I have to say I disagree."

"As you should, given that you're a married woman. And on that note, I must be off. Great nursery, by the way." Leo disappeared toward the front of the store, already shouting something at Zach.

"Phew." Cassie leaned against Ty and closed her eyes. "Are they going to destroy the place while we're gone?"

"Nope." Ty nuzzled her hair. "I had to tell them my secret recipe, though."

"I hope you made them sign a confidentiality agreement."

"Of course. Can't trust those folks at all."

"You think Zach and Leo will ever start to get along?"

"Oh, they love each other. They just don't know it yet."

Cassie snorted. "No way."

"Want to make a wager on that one?"

A stab of pain surged through Cassie. She gasped and hunched forward.

"Cassie! What's wrong?" Ty sounded so alarmed she felt like hugging him.

Which she would do just as soon as she could move again. She held up a finger while she waited for the pain to subside.

"Cassie, talk to me."

Her body finally relaxed and she looked at him. "I think it's time to go to the hospital."

"You're kidding."

"Wouldn't joke about that." It was time!

"Right. We can handle this." He looked sort of pale. "Bags are in the car?"

"I thought you put them there."

"Right, I did." He scooped her up in his arms and began to carry her to the door.

"I can walk, Ty."

"Why walk when I can carry you?"

Why indeed?

She looped her arms around his neck and leaned against him, grinning as he threw the entire shop into a frenzy with a few shouts. Doors opened, hugs were thrown, good wishes showered them.

After Ty settled her in the front seat of his car, he knelt beside her and took her hand. "You ready to become a mom?"

"You bet. And you?"

"No."

"No?"

He shook his head, his eyes twinkling. "I don't want to be a mom. But I can't wait to be a dad." Then he kissed her. "Thanks for making all my dreams come true. Even the ones I didn't know I wanted."

She shrugged. "Forcing you to acknowledge and follow your dreams is my job as your stress management consultant."

"It has nothing to do with love?"

Cassie smiled. "It has everything to do with love."

"And the naked thing?"

"An added bonus."

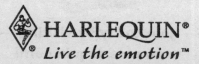

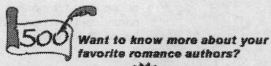

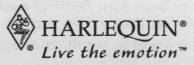